GOING TO NEW ORLEANS

Going to New Orleans

« a dirty book »

CHARLES TIDLER

Anvil Press Publishers | Vancouver

Going to New Orleans
Copyright © 2004 by Charles Tidler

NATIONAL LIBRARY OF CANADA CATALOGUING IN PUBLICATION DATA
Tidler, Charles
Going to New Orleans / Charles Tidler.

ISBN: 1-895636-59-0
I. Title
PS8589.I34G64 2004   C813'.54   C2003-907218-5

Printed and bound in Canada
Cover design: Shawn Shepherd
Typesetting: HeimatHouse

Represented in Canada by the Literary Press Group
Distributed by the University of Toronto Press

The publisher gratefully acknowledges the financial assistance of the B.C. Arts Council, the Canada Council for the Arts, and the Book Publishing Industry Development Program (BPIDP) for their support of our publishing program.

Anvil Press
P.O. Box 3008, Main Post Office
Vancouver, B.C. V6B 3X5 CANADA
www.anvilpress.com

for Tony, Julie,
Natasha—
"way down yonder"

I

"I lost my mind in a wild romance."
— PERCY MAYFIELD

Tulip

Trouble sleeping through the night, shaken awake, still dark, by a dream of a friend of mine and my girlfriend sitting together side by side at the foot of my bed like two angels in a painted picture in The Bible, as if watching over me.

In the dream, he was old, and she was young, and both of them were sad and troubled-looking, with great beneficent concern in their watchful eyes. But then they began to make furious love to each other, and I rose up, wide awake, shocked and shaking, soaking wet in a cold, sour sweat and walked down the hallway to take a pee. There was just enough light from the window to see the bowl without the light on. A robin sang in harmony to the animal joy of my voiding bladder. I was up and wasn't going back to the sack. Not to a dream like that.

A friend of mine, asleep between a foamy and a blanket, took up the middle of my living room floor, and as I stepped over him, he opened his eyes. They were deeply benevolent, as in the dream, and I gasped.

"What's up?" he said.

"Going out," I said.

"What time is it?"

"About five-thirty."

"Put some ice on that eye of yours," he said.

"Yeah, right."

My trumpet lay crushed in the corner by the door. It looked as if someone had run over it with a car.

"Why are you wearing your bicycle helmet?" I said.

But my friend was already asleep again, answering my question with a farty snore. I shut the door behind me and walked down the stairs to the front porch on the main floor of the house and down another set of stairs to the sidewalk.

Plum blossoms drifted like pink snow, blowing down the streets of Victoria. I walked down Moss Street to Dallas Road, the sky becoming blue where seagulls wheel and cry, and a molten, orange Buddha-bubble of sun rises from the black water. Blue mountains. Blue water. I was shivering, hands in pants pockets, refreshed that I was one with a new day, the first day, and not laid out somewhere on some stone tablet stone-dead.

I walked up Beacon Hill and down into the park, still dark, the dark grass soaking in the bright dew, where the crying is peacocks. I walked into a flowerbed, and snapping the stem close to the wet earth, stole a deep purple tulip, before turning and walking out of the park and into James Bay.

I left the tulip in a gumboot on Ms Sugarlicq's enclosed front porch. The screen door latch snapped at my exit. At the corner, I turned and looked back, guilty as salt, shamefully naked, made out of flesh and desire.

Where is my baby this morning?

Where was my baby last night?

I suspected a crisis of spirit about to swallow me as into a whale, and I walked back through the park to a Cook Street coffee shop for the morning papers and a double Americano. I sat by a window, face to face with a madman who stared back at me from the glass, his right eye swollen shut like a split plum.

Like a crushed trumpet.

Like angels screwing at the foot of the bed.

I wanted a clear plan of action, but had only so much with which to work. It was anybody's guess what happened last night and my eye was really beginning to hurt. I pulled a letter from my pocket. It was a contract to go to New Orleans and play in the clubs there for a week in May. I pulled out a pen and signed it.

And down the street past the window the blossoms blew, flowers everywhere, even the clouds in the blue sky foaming like plum blossoms of necessity, fecundity, the sweet, fetid plague of spring, tissues, angels, blossoms running wild in the streets, abandoning consciousness to desire, to the ache of knowing that everything and anything tangible is too beautiful and too free to have any meaning or worth beyond the wasting moment, and yes, yes, yes, especially love, that most fragile flower, just blows away amidst all this flowering.

My name is Lewis King.

I play trumpet.

My girlfriend is insane, and so am I.

Notebook

May 2—
Hanging out a lot with Ms S.

May 3—
All evening with Ms Sugarlicq, who now is playing the game of being nice to me . . . forever the Electric Moment & a good thing. We're going to New Orleans next week.

May 4—
Downpour all day. The erotic show was packed. Long wet line-up under a plastic tarp set up over an outdoor courtyard to keep out the rain, water running down the sides of the plastic, down people's necks, a guy pushing off a big blister of water overhead with a big brush broom. The courtyard dark and wet, swollen with people, barely room to nudge and push slowly through, so many, too many, god damn it's tight in the unpleasantly wet, close space, mildly inhuman . . . but the place calms a bit after a few people panic and leave, and the uncomfortably squishy mass becomes a benign group grope with tequila shooters. Okay.

Dancing til four at a club with Ms S.
Later at home alone with champagne and orange juice.
Pass out in chair.

May 5—

I wake to the beautiful, mad Ms Sugarlicq crawling into my bed with the key to my apartment like a bauble clenched between her teeth. In the sack for three hours. Papers. TV basketball. The rest of the champagne and orange juice. Charmed lifestyle. Cannot protest much.

May 6—

Ms Sugar distant and skittish. She scares me, talking about a night of deceit which she feels somehow obligated to see through to the end, kissing me once off the side of my mouth before disappearing into the night, the lights of the harbour reflecting off the tail of her bicycle.

Beer & Wine store for 6-pack. Stop in at Thursdays Bar for pints, tokes, and hanging out.

Back home. Taped TV basketball.

Drink 6-pack.

Guzzle, guzzle.

Lao Tsu says, "Accept being unimportant."

Pass out in chair.

May 7—

Day of small hell.

Living with bad feelings and total, final darkness.

Confess to a friend over coffee on a bench in the sun in Bastion Square that, for her own safety, Ms S probably ought to be institutionalized immediately.

My friend kindly pats me on the back.

"Did you fuck her?"

"What?" he says.

"Did you fuck her?"

"I'm your number one fan," he says.

"Yeah, right."

"Everything will be fine," he says. "You don't have to kick my bicycle helmet."

Convinced it is a mistake to go to N.O. with Ms S.

Wander down to the Inner Harbour and almost step in front of an ambulance hurtling up Government Street. The attendant riding shotgun points his finger at me.

A block away, a bicycle lies crushed beneath a pickup.

All shook up.

Ms S drops by at my place later, seducing me with a basketball handjob in the chair in front of the TV. Leaves almost immediately, saying she has to go home and pack.

Don't trust her for one second out of my sight.

Go down to Swans for my last gig in Victoria.

Between sets, hang out with the other musicians. Don't want to talk to anybody else.

The guys like my new trumpet.

Have a few pints too many, some laughs, smoke a joint outside on Wharf Street with the bartender.

Fuck the encore.

Go home and drink myself asleep.

May 8—

A good day. The teller at the bank made a mistake, selling me Yankee money at par Canadian.

Ms Sugarlicq comes by, and I feed her supper, halibut steaks, rice, stir fry veg, before popping into the sack for an hour where she insists I spank her, and when I do, she says, "harder, make the flesh pink." And I do.

She wants me to ride home with her, and we do that, going through the dark park on our bicycles, no bike lights on, and she almost loses me. But finally, in the dark trees beside the stone bridge, she waits for me to catch up, her mouth open, pretending we're total strangers, wanting I don't know what, as if waiting for me to . . . speak? kiss? insert my hand like a blade between her legs? I just ride on by until a block later she catches up, flying by, and three blocks of sprinting later we catch our breath together in front of her place. She invites me in and has to show me her packing, every mundane item by item, and she packs in front of me all over again, and then says she wants to be alone.

Frottage
      on the stairs
             descends
                  to cunnilingus.

The sweet Ms Sugarlicq waves goodbye from her second floor window. I wave too and ride my bicycle home where a couple shots of vodka keep me company before bedtime.

Old Boyfriend

On the phone, Ms Sugarlicq said that she has a friend with a car who has offered to drive us out to the airport for free. They could either pick me up at my place, or I can walk a mile and a half with my bag and my trumpet through the park to her place, and we could then walk another three blocks with her three bags and my stuff to a hotel to catch the airporter which is thirteen dollars one way and takes twice the time as a private car.

"Pick me up," I said.

"You would say that," she said.

"Well, who wouldn't?"

"All you ever think about is yourself."

"What the hell are you talking about?"

"This isn't easy for me."

"Going to New Orleans?"

"Picking you up."

"Don't pick me up. Meet me at the airport. Don't meet me at the airport. I don't give a damn. I'm going to New Orleans. Hope to see you there."

I hung up. The phone rang.

"Hello," I said.

"We'll pick you up in five minutes."

"Okay."

"I love you."

"I love you too, baby."

Five minutes later, somebody buzzed my apartment, and a short lopsided wheezing man who looked like a toad was squatting on the steps of the front porch, simultaneously smoking two cigarettes, one in each hand.

"Let me, please, take your bag," he said.

He struggled to get up on his feet and almost fell backwards down the stairs.

"I can manage," I said.

I stepped around him and took the stairs down two at a time to the green front lawn where the sidewalk blazed with sunlight. Clouds like white welts stitched the blue air, and a blustery wind snapped above the plum trees.

"Hi, baby."

She was leaning back in the sun against the front fender of a big-assed, paint-peeling '70s gas pig. She wore cutoffs cut close to her upper thighs and tight up the crack of her ass. A little white scrap of tank top covered her breasts, and her swollen nipples bruised the delicate weave of the cotton.

The fender was hot in the hot sun, and it made her bare flesh look very pink, like uncooked beef at a barbecue. Little beads of golden sweat rolled slowly down the curved bone of her delicate nose.

"Good morning, Ms Sugarlicq," I said.

"Good morning, mister."

"And what brings you out today?"

"Oh, I'm just soaking up the sun like a flesh sponge."

"You might burn."

"I am a reptile."

"Poisonous?"

"I don't know."

"Ravenous?"

"Yes, always."

"Please, let me take that," said the toad.

The lopsided man grabbed for my trumpet case with his right hand which resembled a pair of wire cutters, and I wrestled with him as with a lobster over a basket, finally pulling the case away, causing him to lose his balance and fall to the ground.

"I'll look after my own stuff, thank you," I said.

The toad huffed and puffed on the ground and rolled around, whimpering pathetically, like a bloated, human garbage bag.

"Kick him," said Ms Sugarlicq.

"I'm not going to kick him," I said.

"Fuck you," she said.

Ms Sugarlicq opened the car door and got in. It was a four-door.

"You're in the back," she said.

She turned her head and wouldn't look at me.

"Help me up," said the toad.

"Help yourself," I said.

I almost kicked him.

"Go ahead," he said.

I opened the back door and got into the car, sitting directly behind Ms S, behind all her shiny hair and her dark sighing. The trumpet case was on my lap.

"Who is this guy?"

"An old boyfriend."

"I guess they come in handy sometimes."

"You're the one getting the free ride to the airport."

"What did you get?"

"I got laid. Does that make you happy?"

The toad pried open the driver's door and got in, the wire cutters taking the wheel.

"We better get a move on," he said.

Ms Sugarlicq yawned.

Spark plugs fired, and the gas pig sped away down the street.

A block and a half later, we ran a red light.

"That was a red light," I said.

The toad turned around in his seat and looked at me.

"What?" he said.

"Don't look at me," I said. "You're driving the fucking car."

The toad turned back in time to avoid an onrushing bus. Horns blared, and from behind I could hear a large crash of metal and glass. The gas pig skidded to the right.

"I know a shortcut," said the toad.

He turned us down an alley.

A siren flared and then was lost in the sharp and flashing chaos of the rushing, crystal city. The toad ran four stop lights in succession, narrowly missing three more head-on collisions, but soon we were cruising at a modest hundred klicks in the thick highway traffic swim to the airport, and I thought if we didn't get killed en route, we might make it to our flight on time.

"Oh, baby, the way you sat on my face last night," said the toad.

He smacked his lips and grunted, much the way Ms Sugarlicq grunts when she comes.

"Shut up," said Ms S.

She hissed it out like a snake.

"Oh, baby, you lick my balls like licking an ice cream cone," said the toad.

He laughed the way she laughs.

Ms Sugarlicq slapped his face, and her bloodred index fingernail sliced an inch of flesh, thin as a broken red pencil's sharpened lead, bleeding across his right cheek.

"Oh, baby," cried the toad. "I come for you, I bleed for you."

He licked at the trickle of blood with his tongue.

"I scar for you, baby."

Ms Sugarlicq rolled her left hand into a tight fist and hit him with three quick short jabs to the jaw, and the car almost went off the road.

The wire cutters wrestled with the wheel.

"You hurt me, baby," he said.

We ran yet another red light.

I could hear another siren.

The toad caught his breath the way Ms Sugarlicq catches hers.

"I think you broke my jaw," he said.

The toad hurled us toward another red light.

"It hasn't stopped you from talking," she said.

The left turn lane to the airport was clear, and its turning arrow light flashed green.

"This is our turn," I said.

The toad fishtailed through a yellow light going red, and we were on the airport road.

"Take me with you, baby," he said.

His voice cracked, and he swallowed a blubbering gob.

"Take me with you, baby," he said.

"This is departures," I said.

The toad hit the brake, and we jerked to a stop.

The lopsided man dropped his large head to the steering wheel and began to sob.

"Take me with you, baby," he said.

"Get over it," said Ms S.

She opened the door and got out of the car.

The toad banged his forehead repeatedly against the steering wheel.

"No, no, no, no, no," he said.

I opened my door and got out.

I helped Ms Sugarlicq pull her three bags from the trunk.

The driver's door popped open, and the toad huffed and puffed, trying to squeeze himself off the front seat of the gas pig.

"Let's run," she said.

Ms Sugar stepped from the street to the sidewalk, but the velvet strap on her left high heel snapped, her ankle twisted slightly, and she dropped two of her bags.

"I got them," I said.

I wrestled her three big bags plus my own into my arms.

Ms S bent down to repair the torn strap, and the toad stumbled into her from behind, falling down on his face on the sidewalk. Blood spilled from his forehead and the bridge of his nose, blood on the sidewalk, dripping down his arms and on his hands. The toad threw his arms around Ms Sugarlicq's right leg and held on.

Ms S screamed.

"Take me with you, baby," he said.

She took two steps toward the terminal, dragging him along, and then stopped and looked at me.

"Kick him," she said.

I put down the bags, walked up to the toad and kicked him as hard as I could in the soft spot just below the sternum. He let go of Ms S and rolled around, trying to breathe again.

Ms S walked away, more lovely than ever despite the broken strap, or perhaps in irony because of it, a savage, blonde goddess almost floating—yes, floating through the automatic doors into Departures.

The toad, on hands and knees, was crawling away to his car.

I picked up the four bags and the trumpet case.

I didn't look back.

Passports

My passport measures $3^{7/16}$ inches by $4^{7/8}$ inches (88MM x 125MM). It is navy blue. It has twenty-four pages. The front cover says, "PASSPORT" and "United States of America" and in between is the seal of the USA. On the inside front cover is a black and white photo of myself. It measures $1^{1/2}$ inches by $1^{3/8}$ inches (45MM x 35MM). Beside the photo is my surname and my given names. My nationality is United States of America. There's also my date of birth, place of birth, date of issue of the passport, date of expiration (almost ten years hence) and by what authority.

Ms Sugarlicq forgot her passport and didn't think to pack her birth certificate.

"You could be denied entry into the United States," said the woman at the Air Canada desk.

"What?" said Ms. Sugarlicq.

"Next," said the woman.

A Glass of Beer

I sat on a stool in a Vancouver airport bar. In front of me was a coaster but not a drink, and that was okay because I was trying hard to accept being unimportant. But if I did have in my hand the beer that I'm waiting for, I would drink to the kindness of strangers in uniform, even to the last American asshole on the planet.

A US customs guard told Ms Sugarlicq that her driver's licence card, her CareCard and her SIN card were all cards also in the billfold of the Hindu cab driver sitting outside the terminal waiting for a fare downtown. What the Hindu cab driver didn't have was a passport card or a birth certificate card, and neither did Ms Sugarlicq.

"That's a racist comment," I said, my voice barely a whisper, dropping it like a chewing gum wrapper to the carpet at my feet so the customs guard wouldn't hear me.

"He's not a racist," said Ms S. "He was just explaining."

The customs guard smiled.

"My job is to protect the sovereignty of The United States of America," he said, still smiling.

Ms Sugar's chin began to tremble. She would soon cry.

A little ragged leer hung to the edge of the smile of the customs guard like a fresh chancre sore. It said—*got you—I*

just took a picture of your pussy with an x-ray camera.
He let her in.
Gate E86.
Going to Chicago.

Ah, here it is, and I have now a fresh glass of dark beer at hand. A heart-shaped thumb print melts into the frosted glass, and Ms Sugarlicq comes up from behind. She puts her arms around my chest and kisses the back of my neck with a little bite that squeezes the skin tight as a needle's stitch.

"Delicious."

"The beer?" she said laughing, or more like some kind of low-rumbling grunt mixing with laughter. Can you grunt and laugh at the same time?

"I can feel your nipples in my back."

Again, Sugarlicq grunted.

"I'm going to make it all up to you."

"I'm sure that you will."

The waitress said, "Can I get you anything?"

"I just want this man."

"He's a lucky man," said the waitress and walked away.

"Baby, I'm flying to Chicago, and thank god you're coming too," I said.

"If you want me, I'm coming too."

I finished my beer, one dark bittersweet gulp, and shrugged my shoulders, dropping them back down slowly across delicate cotton tight to her still-erect nipples.

Mile High Club

Six miles high, and contented as a fatting cow in a corn field, Ms Sugarlicq burps, farts, snores and sleeps over all of green Iowa. She dreams of crossing the Mississippi in a gold plated frying pan, a silver spoon for a paddle. Her prairie, fairytale world is one vast newly-mown Illinois. The cows chew, the boys plow, and the girls dance in the popping corn. My baby's going to river bend, going to river's end, her wet bottom, wet pussy, going, going to New Orleans.

Ms Sugarlicq curls up into a ball, against the airplane window's hard plastic pillow of yellow sun. Her eyes close, and she grunts when I put my index finger up to my nose to smell her come. She grunts and jerks her head back hard against the window glass, slumps off to sleep again.

"Sink."

The woman sitting beside me in the aisle seat fans the air with a *Newsweek.*

"Sink?"

"Stink," she says.

I put on headphones and tune in channel 09.

Oscar Peterson at Carnegie Hall.

"Strangers in the night . . ."

But the strange woman has her hands on my crotch. She's

squeezing my cock and balls, and I sit up. The woman looks me in the eye and screams, but squeezes my balls once more before letting go. She jumps out of her seat and bumps into a stewardess. They exchange a few words in rapid fire Spanish, and the woman pushes the stewardess aside.

"Stink," she says in English and stumbles out of sight down the aisle.

I sit up straight and remember to breathe again.

My pants are tight and wet.

My cock is hard.

I shake my head, slap my face.

Next to me, Ms Sugarlicq contentedly snores.

Ella sings, "*Anything Goes.*"

I walk up the aisle to get in line for a restroom.

The OCCUPIED bar slides to VACANT, the restroom door pushes open, and the woman steps out. When she sees me, she looks back and sniffs the air.

She winks.

"Stink," she says, and laughs.

I shrug, pretending I don't know what she's talking about.

"Next," she says, and laughs again.

She holds the door for me.

"Thank you."

I step into the restroom.

Somebody kidney-punches me from behind. I gasp and jerk forward, bumping my head against the wall above the toilet bowl. A body squeezes in behind me. It's the woman.

I hear the door close and lock.

The lights come on.

She reaches from behind and unzips my pants, taking my cock and balls into her two soft hands, squeezing my sack like nuts in velvet gloves, her thumbs spiraling, two plump flames, entwine the rigid vine, and I begin to shudder.

"Stink," she says.

I come into her small hands.

I catch my breath.

I can see her in the mirror, rubbing come over her taciturn face, through her jet black hair. She catches my eye.

"Skin," she says. "You good skin."

"Skin?"

The door pops open, the lights go out.

"Good stink," she says, laughing, and she's gone.

I lock the door again.

The lights come on.

I press down on the flat aluminum lever of the cold water tap and proceed with my ablutions.

Three Cigarettes

Just outside the ground floor of Terminal Two at Chicago's O'Hare Airport, there's a dirty little park full of dogshit and cigarette butts. In the park are two small trees, poor abused urban angels, sickly green, and both with broken limbs hanging down to the ground. They take the heat of the day like a lashing. The park has gardens but no flowers, and a low, pale yellow greenish hedge runs around it like the thickening, foamy boundary of something in a toilet bowl.

Clad in a skintight white jumpsuit, Ms Sugarlicq turns cartwheels on the filthy lawn. Dark, damp triangles of sweat blossom beneath both arms, between her legs, three spinning spots; she flips, jumps, somersaults, crisscrossing space and time and dogshit in the draining, killing sun.

Cabs drive by and honk.

Ms Sugarlicq stands on her head, bringing her feet slowly down, sole to sole, showing all of Chicago an idealized representation of the one, perfectly wet white orchid of pussy.

A man in a cowboy hat collapses on the sidewalk.

He clutches his heart.

Somebody runs to a telephone.

Ms Sugarlicq stretches and yawns like a cat.

Ms Sugarlicq reclines.

She smokes, in rapid succession, three cigarettes.

A small crowd of men has gathered in the park. They mill about like sniffing dogs.

"Get up," I say.

I hold out my right hand to her. I want to help her stand up, but she won't do it.

She shakes her head.

"Go away," she says.

"You don't want to sit in all this shit," I say.

The park is full of men standing around in dogshit.

"I want to fuck every man I meet," she says. "You're nobody special."

Here am I in a dirty little park, looking askance into the filthy sky, and in the distance there's a long row of flagpoles each with an American flag snapping in the thin, hot sun. The first one snaps, and then each succeeding flag snaps in the sky like a whip, a welting, slicing string of snaps, and I, a naked slave to love in the full bite of the savage sun, beg each raw strip of steak across my own unworthy, naked back.

Chicago All Dressed Hot Dog

Chicago is the home of big shoulders, the fog on cat's feet, and plainspoken people. Chicago is the home of electric blues. Muddy Waters, Little Walter, Junior Wells. Guys who could fill up a room. And Chicago is the home of the all beef, all dressed hot dog.

So I wanted to eat a Chicago hot dog and was looking around the airport for a place where I could get one. I walked from one end of the terminal to the other, walking past all the places where you could eat and finally walked into a restaurant bar and sat at a table with a menu, and when the waitress came around I ordered a Chicago hot dog.

"We don't serve hot dogs," she said.

"I didn't want to hear you say that," I said.

"We have buns, but we don't have hot dogs."

"Your buns are going to get lonely."

"You think so?" she said.

"Yes," I said.

"That's so sad."

"True. Sad and blue."

"I might be able to help you."

"You might?"

"Yes, I might."

"I could use a little help."

"I know where you can get a hot dog."

"You do?"

"Yes, I do."

"A Chicago hot dog?"

"Extra large?"

"Yes."

"Polish sausage?"

"Yes."

"All beef?"

"Yes."

"All dressed?"

"Yes, yes, oh, god, yes."

"Follow me, honey," she said.

She took me by the hand and led me like a child from the restaurant back into the flow of the terminal and pointed me down the long aisle to a destination I couldn't quite see.

"A yellow cart with a yellow awning?"

"Colour hot mustard," she said.

"You are so sweet."

"They will satisfy your every need for a Chicago hot dog."

"Thank you."

"For everything else, you'll have to come back here."

"Everything and anything?"

"Any way you want it."

"Except a Chicago hot dog."

"Well, you go and get yourself one."

"I will."

"Then you be ready for some pie."

She laughed. She winked and wiggled her bottom, and I almost followed her back into the restaurant bar.

But the hot dog stand was everything I had hoped for and more. The staff was courteous and friendly, going way over the top to ensure and enhance the sensual pleasures of purchasing and consuming their product, the all beef, all dressed, Chicago hot dog.

"Mustard?"

"Hot mustard, please."

"Mayo?"

"Sure."

"Onions?"

"Yes."

"Tomatoes?"

"Yes."

"Lettuce?"

"Yes."

"Relish?"

"Yes."

"Peppers?"

"Yes."

"Pickles?"

"Yes."

"Sweet?"

"Yes."

"Dill?"

"Yes."

"Bread and butter?"

"Yes."

"Hot peppers?"

"Yes."

"Hot salsa?"

"Yes."

"Cucumber?"

"Yes."

"That's one all dressed dog."

"All right, and thank you."

I had at last in my hand the perfect hot dog, a Chicago

all dressed, for less than four dollars American, and I was going to eat it with great pleasure.

"Can I have a bite?" said Ms Sugarlicq.

The tip of her tongue licked my left ear.

"Sure," I said.

I handed her the perfect dog.

She took a big bite.

"Oh, that's so good," she said, chewing.

"Where have you been?"

"Talking to a baggage handler," she said.

"Your bags are checked through to New Orleans."

"We weren't talking about bags."

"Oh."

"Can I have another bite?"

She took a second big bite.

"This is so good," she said, chewing.

"What were you talking about?"

"Who?"

"The baggage handler."

"We weren't talking."

"So, you just had sex with a baggage handler?"

"No."

She took a third bite.

"Just a blowjob," she said, chewing.

She offered the remains of the dog.

"No, thank you."

"You amaze me," she said.

She threw the half-eaten dog into a garbage can, the white paper napkin and the white cardboard paper cradle—its dirty bottom greased and yellow-stained with mustard, a visually awkward and pathetic triviality—falling with the impact of skull and brains suddenly struck by a blunt instrument, a freefalling dead weight in a slaughterhouse democracy of bovine intestines, hooves, feces, hair, death, sex, death, all spiraling through the steel screw meat grinder maw of the teeth mother.

"And *you* amaze me," I said.

Sugar Pie Fizz

En route Chicago to New Orleans.

The sun, burnt orange, glazes the curve of the earth, and the Mississippi River is a bold black snake in the dark. The river towns flash like fireworks, and a bridge across the sprawling river is a necklace of fire.

" . . . Sugar pie, honey bunch . . ."

Everybody in the 727 chatting and laughing, eating ham and cheese, Fritos chips, flirting with the tightass steward and the big-titted stewardess.

" . . . I'm in love with you . . ."

"Would you like cream in your coffee?"

"Yes, please," I say.

"I'd like your cream in me," says Ms Sugar, darting her tongue, rapid fire, in and out, fucking my right ear, the little white hairs going first rigid and then curling with electrical pleasure.

" . . . Can't help myself . . ."

The senses come alive, sexual motors purring, and my physical body decomposes, shatters and explodes, ending somewhere below the shoulders. From there on down, consciousness is a carbonated fizz of sensual anticipation.

"We're going to New Orleans, baby," I say.

"I know we are," says Ms Sugar.

" . . . I love you & nobody else . . ."

The stewardess is handing out blankets, and Ms S, pouting, begs for one, pretty, pretty please, and spreads the baby-blue wool across our laps.

"Hang on," I say.

"You hang on."

Ms Sugarlicq dives beneath the blanket, nudging her head into my lap. The button on my pants pops open, and the zipper slides away.

"Oh," I say.

And Jack is out of his box.

" . . . Sugar pie, honey bunch . . ."

"Oh," I say.

"Is everything all right?" says the stewardess.

She bends over me with a curiously benign smile, but I don't register the logic of her statement because I'm looking down her dress where two full breasts like bunnies nest in pure white cotton.

"You're okay?" says the stewardess, bending closer, her nipples like hard, dark berries. Close enough I can smell her mix of sweat and perfume.

"Yes," I say.

I try to say it without shaking.

"Oh god," I say.

« 36 »

" . . . I'm in love with you . . ."

"If you need anything," says the stewardess.
My body shudders.

" . . . Can't help myself . . ."

Going, going, going to New Orleans.

II

II

Professor New Orleans

Doc Nawlins, my booking agent in New Orleans, picks us up in his limo, a '70s rustbucket Datsun, at the airport about 10 p.m., and we motor, hysterical with anticipation, madcap adrenalin, drifting green cloud of stinky pot, roaring down historic Highway 61, the roadway to fame for Muddy Waters, Bob Dylan, Louis Armstrong ... *"Baby, please don't go, baby, please don't go, back to New Orleans because I love you so"* ... passing a pint of Wild Turkey back and forth and back and forth. Crescent City, The Big Easy, baby, nonstop honking laughter, wicked, evil, once running a fucking red light—jesus, Doc, they don't want to hear me in this town that bad. My heart thumping against my shirt like an abused caged animal, like mortality taking its grip on the back of my neck and shoving me facefirst into an unforgiving mirror that slices the throat cleanly; catching my breath, roaring, hitting every pothole on St Charles Avenue ... finally, mercy, mercy, turning onto a side street to the Doc's place in Uptown, crawling out of the Datsun as if from a car wreck, in front of an old house with a dirty yellow cloud of noseeums on the little front porch, a house of small rooms and high ceilings, painted black and white and blood-red. And we drank beer, Abita Red, and talked, chattering like monkeys over bananas, about food, beer, and music, and sex—what else is there in New Orleans? Doc puts on a

Robert Johnson CD . . . "*Squeeze my lemon, the juice running down my leg*" . . . and he and Ms. Sugarlicq get to know each other, the two of them dancing around the living room floor like deadly spiders coming in for the kill, trading tongues and innuendo, Doc unzipping his trousers unannounced, his cock straight as a shovel handle, swinging like a metronome, and Ms Sugarlicq down on her knees, swallows his cock whole, gulp and gurgle and gasp and groan, and Doc, between moans, begs me to open, open, please, a couple more bottles of Abita Red, and he and Ms S roll around on the living room carpet like two dogs stuck together in an alley, double-backed, wailing with pain and pleasure. Oh, and I'm tired and dirty, tired and dirty and shitty and dirty, and Doc shouts out, angry as a master over his dog, ordering me to crack open beer after beer after beer, and finally, hours, days, a week later I'm lowering my face into a toilet bowl's oval simplicity of pooled water and porcelain, so cold, so white, so pure, and something low in my insides begins to pump up, pump up, pump up through my throat, gathering momentum, pumps up out of my mouth, a pumping fountain of puke and ham and cheese and bread and hot dog and cucumber and sour onions and bile and jealous rage. It pumps up, pumps out in chunks of pink and green excess, *rip, rip, rip,* god knows what happens next, *rip,* finally someone, *rip,* Ms Sugarlicq, or Doc, now dressed in a dress, or my own double mistaken in a shroud of mirrors, someone, who I don't know, *rip,* suggests I go to bed, *rip,* and I'm led by someone, led like a stressed—and freaked out—but an amazingly and ironically self-aware and docile cow, *moo,* into the slaughterhouse of jealous love. Oh, please, spare me, into a bedroom, there's a bed and pillows and blankets, an air conditioner whining like a chainsaw, and I'm undressing, one pant leg at a time, one sock at a time. I'm laughing, laughing, falling on my face, laughing, shit, fresh blood and vomit, and I'm cursing, *fuck, fuck,* and a hand takes me by the hand, this way, love, you don't have to swear, and it's Ms Sugarlicq helping me up. I'm staggering, weaving back and forth, she's showing me the way to bed. I'm falling in, and a pillow catches me like the bayou catches a waterlogged tree, the ceiling spinning, the floor dissolving, my guts erupting, brain collapsing into the depths of Hell, spinning, spinning, spinning, Ms Sugarlicq is licking my cock . . . blackout?

Streetcar Dreams

I'm in bed but can't sleep. Across the bed, not touching, Ms Sugarlicq tosses around in the throes of masturbating. She shudders, stills, sighs, and then throws her body on top of me.

"Grease me up, daddy," she says.

I stick my middle finger in her pussy.

"Grease my slide," she says.

She grinds against my hand for a moment, suddenly changes her mind, rolls away, and a few moments later is all over me again until we ravish each other in a vigorous sixty-nine.

I drift off to sleep . . . waking later, she's standing at the foot of the bed in a white nightgown. A sweet little angel, spreading her wings . . . and there's another figure beside her, a middle-aged man with a white beard wearing a blue bicycle helmet.

"What are you doing here?" I say.

"I'm your fan club, Lewis," he says, and he fades . . . blue and white smoke.

I sit up, panting, from a shocking dream.

She crawls into bed, I touch her, and she throws my hand away. I move to the edge of the bed and try to fall asleep again . . . the birds, exotic and warm, close by in the dark heat, warble and coo from the oak trees black as the night, and every once in a while a block away the St Charles Avenue streetcar passes, and the house and the bed shake, rocking, a gentle rhythmical mechanical railroad rocking, a repetitive, lowgrade but soothing rumble. A streetcar passing stirs Ms Sugarlicq, and turning over, her hand takes my cock up, begins to pump in rhythm with the rocking . . . I grew up in a train town, right beside the tracks, and the rhythm, all the rocking, floats me . . . coming and going and drifting and rocking to sleep.

But Ms S wakes me.

She's waving her pillow in the air, and in my face.

"What are you doing?" I say.

"Your farts smell bad," she says.

"Oh, christ, grow up," I say.

Falling back to sleep . . . birds . . . streetcar dreams . . . rocking, rocking, rocking . . .

Public Works Dept

"Suck it, bitch, suck it."
"Oh, oh, oh."
"Suck it."
"Oh."
"Suck it."
"Oh."
"Suck."
"Oh, yes."
"Oh, baby."
"Yes, yes, yes."

I twist, waking bolt upright from a nightmare. I'm in bed alone, looking around the empty room. I can hear water running through two closed doors, the shower in the bathroom. There's sand between the sheets, and I get up and shake them off, and most of the sand dances to the foot of the bed, but not enough of it for me to want to get back in.

Beside the bed is an open window, humid daylight and street voices, and I take a look outside where workmen dick around on the broken, sandy street, leaning on a yellow backhoe, telling stories. The backhoe is parked in the middle of the torn-up street. Apparently they're in no hurry to do anything resembling work soon. One guy squeals. He slides in the sand in the middle of the street like a six-year-old boy playing baseball.

"She licked dick," he says.

He rolls his head around on his shoulders, walks like a rooster.

"On a roof," he says.

He points at me in the window.

"That's him."

I step behind the curtain.

I can hear him laughing.

I look again.

He's turning a back-flip off the bucket of the backhoe.

"They he is," he says. "The man with horns."

He puts his hands up to the sides of his head, the index fingers curling upwards.

He laughs.

He dances in the sand.

And that's when I notice the ladder for the first time, an aluminum extension ladder that is stamped with letters in blue paint: Property of the City of New Orleans, Public Works Dept, leaning up against the roof of the house just beneath the window, and the ends of the ladder, too, are in the air like two horns sticking up.

Grits and Fried Bread

The day was sunny and hot and muggy, and I was spread eagle, flat on my back on the bedroom floor, immobile, painfully hungover, but trying to be positive and think about good things, like how much I love this kind of weather, like how lucky I am to be alive, and at last, desiring this and that pleasure of the flesh, I decided to make a move.

I looked around on hands and knees for my underwear, a pair of shorts and a T-shirt, and got dressed. The shower in the bathroom was still going steady, but, oh, I didn't dare walk in there where a savage, wild she-beast was very likely licking her wounds, her rosy rows of bites, lists of slights, vague feelings of self-pity, pity poor me, a pitiful delicate flower bathing her milkwhite skin with rosemary, pity, purity and oil.

No, never go in there.

I would be too easy, vulnerable prey.

Do not choose this door.

I opened the bathroom door and stepped into steam.

"What the hell is going on?" I said.

Ms Sugarlicq pulled back the shower curtain. She was scrubbing her pussy with a loofah sponge.

"I hate you, go away," she said.

She pulled the shower curtain closed.

"Were you fucking around with a workman?" I said.

"What?"

"The guys working in the street," I said.

"Fuck you," she said.

I pulled back the shower curtain. I grabbed her left arm.

"Let go of me," she said.

"Bend over," I said.

I smacked her wet ass on the right cheek as hard as I could with my open palm.

She squealed.

"I hate you."

"You be a good girl," I said.

"I don't have to."

"I'll put you on the next plane back to Canada."

"That's not fair."

She pulled the shower curtain closed.

"You're a bad man," she said.

"Right."

"There's a red mark on me," she said.

"Good."

I closed the bathroom door and stood there, listening through the door to the shower. My right hand was still stinging.

Downstairs, I found Doc in the kitchen in his housecoat, stirring with a wooden spoon a pot of grits and shaved cheese, all of it burning, congealing slowly and irreversibly into a yellow doughball of fat and corn. The burning is part of the charm. He's got fried bread burning on the stove top, and the bittersweet burnt stench of chicory coffee on the go, bubbling through an automatic machine, the shiny black liquid oily and hot in a clean glass pot.

"Later make some groceries," Doc said.

"Always pick up a couple po'boys somewhere," I said.

"Want to get some long necks in here."

"Quart of that Wild Turkey."

"Turbo Dogs."

"Bread pudding with praline sauce."

"Sweet potato pie."

"So, where I playing?"

"Anywhere, every . . . every . . ."

Doc must think something's funny, he can't finish his sentence because he's laughing so hard.

"Don't hurt yourself," I said.

"Oh, my, you have some fun, Lewis."

I talked with Doc, drank a cup of Louisiana style chicory coffee with steamed milk and cane sugar, talked about life and music and sex and New Orleans . . . while from upstairs in the bedroom, if I strained my ear, I could hear voices coming down the stairs.

"Shh," I said.

"Just a little bit."

"No, no, no, no, no."

It's Ms S scolding someone.

"What?" Doc said.

"It's that god damn workman," I said.

"I'll get my gun," Doc said.

I went outside, down the walk and around to the front of the house. The workman was on the roof, pleading with Ms Sugarlicq in the bedroom window. I grabbed the aluminum ladder. It shook in my hands.

"Hey," the workman said.

I wrestled the ladder, forcing it to fall to the ground where it crashed hard, rattling at my feet, stabbing its cuckold-like prongs into the innocent lawn.

"That property the city," he said.

The bedroom window opened. Doc Nawlins leaned out, waving a gun.

"How's your momma and dem?" said the workman.

He took a step forward, his arms spread, and stumbled. The gun in Doc Nawlins's hand barked twice, the workman jerked up, and in slow motion flipped backwards head over heels off the roof, hitting the ground with a hard thud. He rolled over twice, and I had to jump back to avoid being hit.

The workman arched his back and got up, wobbling but on his feet again. He pulled his cock from his pants and began to vigorously masturbate, come jetting out like a stream of milk across the ladder, and then, confused, vaguely self-reflectively unsure of himself, he let go his grip, his eyes snapped shut, his whole body curled slowly backwards into a grotesque, inhuman rainbow shape, shaking, retching, reaching, recklessly spastic, then crawling on his belly like a snake, with one hand extended toward the ladder which was the property of the City of New Orleans, his left index finger almost, but not quite, touching the fuzzy end of a frayed strand of quarter-inch, yellow polyethylene rope that was entwined and tied fast with bowline knots around the serrated rungs of the aluminum ladder. This gesture was seemingly without substance or purpose, symbolizing nothing but a complete and meaningless end to what he had more than likely been led to believe by the Dept of Public Works in the Parish of Orleans to be a life worthy not only of spiritual salvation leading to the gates of paradise . . . "thank you, jesus" . . . but a life that, with a little effort on his part, like coming to work mostly every morning and staying all day most of the time, would also be blessed with a nice fat pension. But no, that's not going to happen, not the pension part anyway. Sorry, pal . . . "Lord, have mercy on my wicked soul" . . . amen, and then the workman, like film set afire, like futile despair, crumpled into an unmoving, lifeless lump of dead meat that in the humid heat is already beginning to stink. A small, spent sack of steaming shit taking up space on the blue and green earth for no apparent reason.

River Run

Doc Nawlins loans us bicycles, and Ms Sugarlicq and I race
along the top of the levee, past riverside vegetable stands
where you can buy Cajun tomatoes, red and delicious and
falling apart in your hands, cucumbers green and straight
and sweet with starbursting seed, sweet potatoes big as a fist,
fat and stiff and hard . . .
      racing by humble squatter shacks
shyly hiding in the deep green mosses and willows of the
mud flats, shacks built on poles with swaying boardwalks a
watery tickle above the muscle of the river, shacks built of
threadbare hope and rusting corrugated tin dreams . . .
      we're racing by, racing each other,
laughing and shouting and singing, racing the wind and the
water, the time and the day, trying to keep pace with the
mighty brown river, brown god, rushing to the sea, blue and
green world, blue and green and brown, the white clouds
above blowing through space, the afternoon running away
towards the evening . . .
      racing rusty freighters, oil drum
barges, railroad cars, steel bridges, tugboats flexing muscle,
industry smoking and shitting, power towers, wasted
ground, abandoned razor wire, a twisting, twisted, working

river of commerce and blunt poetry, river of song and sleep and dream, exotic, muddy, powerful, ever changing, flowing and flowering and renewing life as it passes, time and the river, dreams and the river, one process of becoming and leaving behind, this is is this . . .

I'm following her lovely behind, oh, give me a moment to linger, leering at her perfect, pear-shaped butt on a high bicycle seat, no one's handing me this, I'm pedaling hard, keeping up close enough to smell the fine blonde hairs at the nape of her neck, sweet as the tender green fiddleheads at the headwaters of the Mississippi River . . .

up in Minnesota where the waters begin blue as sky stirring, where the red-winged blackbird sings, where the swallow carves the riverbank sand, and a lover's finger follows along the spine, like a slow pad-dle-wheeler, every undulating turn of the river, every twisting brown surge of water, every bridge, every smokestack, every shallow of hyacinths, a three thousand-mile twisting knot of detritus and paradox and black-eyed Susans, big muddy, the old man, old nosegay, cow carcasses and daisies and railroad cars flowing big brown at river bend . . .

getting off the bicycles, we run down the side of the steep green levee, going all the way down deep into the wet delta bottom to pull up the whole meaning of life by the roots, soaking wet, we step without thinking into the soft mud at the edge of the purple hyacinths . . .

blue and purple and iris, the colours of origami tissue paper, delicate as lavender labial open-ings, opening from the flower within, a yellow spot of erectile flame, opening to silken pistils of swimming sperm, the hyacinth profuse amid the green of the shal-low mud flats like ten thousand purple butterflies, flitting, flying, alighting, purple butterflies with sturdy green anchors in the muddy earth . . .

the hyacinth gives up the mud like a lover coming, the root squealing like a fat weaner pig, I pull the whole plant up, my shoes sinking in the wet mud, filling with muddy water, water mixed with shit and laughter and blood and mud, coming to river bend, coming to river's end, river run, river run . . .

pulling Miss Sugarlicq down into the shallow wet-lands, wrestling her down like a shiny fish, like a large water bird, wild alligator, a Cajun mermaid, Voodoo river queen, tearing at her silk panties, pulling them down wet below her knees, freeing an ankle with my teeth, flash of wet burgundy silk, her wet bottom coming into sweetness next to the bone, making love in the mud to my lover like the river fucks a flower . . .

A Little Nap

Ride for miles along the river . . . Ms S takes some pictures, and we ride back . . . she suddenly stopping in the middle of the asphalt path atop the levee. I almost rearend her, and a couple of joggers have to step off quickly into the pale dry grass at the edge of the steep bank to pass by.

"What the hell are you doing?" I say.

"I don't want to go out with you and Doc to the clubs tonight," she says.

"Fine. Just don't try to kill me in the meantime."

"I'm a free agent," she says.

"Okay, so am I."

She jumps on her bike like a cat and begins to pedal away hard.

"I came to play," I say.

She hears me. She turns around. She dismounts and hangs her head. Her bike falls to the ground.

I walk up to her.

"What's going on?" I say.

"You can fuck me up the ass," she says.

We ride some more, side by side, stop to buy water at a corner deli on St Charles Avenue, and continue lakeside against traffic past Loyola's "Touchdown Jesus," and turn riverside crossing neutral ground into the oak tree groves of Audubon Park, riding past the zoo, and on top of Audubon's bronze statue, a songbird is singing crazy ... singing *"you can't shoot me, John James Audubon"* ... and again we ride beside the river.

The sunlight blazes the surface of the water like something hammered, and we stop to rest under a tree of doily shade where a squirrel drops pieces of bark on my head ... and Ms Sugar is laughing.

An old couple walk by on the banquette running along the levee. The river, muddy and brown and wide, full of freight and craft, passes behind them. A freighter is sinking, a helicopter is going down. Sirens begin to wail.

"Hello," the lady says.

"Hello," I say.

"It's an easy life," the gentleman says.

"It sure is," I say.

"Yeah, you right," the lady says.

It's almost four o'clock and we're hungry. We ride along the river again, and then up to Maple Street, looking for a place to eat ... but every place we see looks dirty to Ms Sugar. Finally she says she's confused and wants to go back to Doc's. There we find some carrots, an apple, a tin of yogurt. I pop open an Abita Red, eating and drinking together on the porch stoop. The ladder is still in the yard, bordered by police tape and four stakes driven into the ground.

"Let's go back inside, baby," I say.

We get up and go inside, and I close the door on the police tape yard. We listen to some Bill Evans ... *"I Love You"* ... and kiss and hug for a few minutes on the living room couch. I undo the buttons on her pants and put my hand down inside her panties, her pussy soft and wet around my fingers.

"Take anything you want," she says.

I lick my wet fingers, tasting her like licking ice cream.

"I love you," she says.

"I love you, too, baby," I say.

"I need you," she says.

"Let's go upstairs and have a nap," I say.

We go upstairs, take off our clothes and lie down on the bed.

I start to kiss her.

"Let's turn off the air conditioner," she says.

"Okay, but it feels kind of good."

She gets up, turns it off and lies back down.

I start to kiss her.

She pulls away.

"What's going on?" I say.

"Everything changes between us when we take our clothes off," she says.

"Yeah, like we're naked," I say.

"I have to look at you," she says.

"What the hell is this about?"

"You murdered a man," she says.

"Did not."

"You took his ladder away," she says.

She begins to cry.

"Fuck. You don't know shit about it," I say.

"Why do you swear all the time?" she says.

"Stop blubbering."

"Your mother didn't breastfeed you," she says.

"But she taught me how to drink."

I get up, start putting on my pants.

"Come back to bed."

"I thought I murdered a man."

"It kind of turns me on."

I laugh.

"Masturbate," I say.

She takes hold of her mons with her right hand, the middle finger bent like a three-jointed fishing rod, and dips into her pussy, folding, unfolding, refolding the upper fleshy tissues, turning quickly, quicker, quick, quick counterclockwise tiny tight circles . . . circles turning, quick, quick, jerking her head back, mouth trembling, she begins to slowly, lowly moan, a tone deeply bronzed like some sadly beautiful curved horn braying in a snowy, jungle temple at dawn . . . moaning sadly, a deeply open black and white and bronze sorrow . . . the bent finger begins turning blue, turning purple, pumping blood to a fingernail needlepoint of pleasure and pain, pain, pleasure, pleasure, pain.

"Oh, oh, oh," she says.

Her right hand jerks and rises like a bird taking flight in the air. Her pussy is an open rose soaking in a puddle of creamy come.

"Is that what you wanted, baby?" she says.

Her blue finger is turning pink again, to *a look of belonging there as has the flush upon sunset clouds.*

"Yeah, something like that."

Something like pleasure and something like pain. Something like a woman at peace, floating in orgasm.

Making Some Groceries

Doc Nawlins comes home with some groceries, and we start drinking from a quart of Wild Turkey.

I clean my trumpet at the kitchen table.

"Good to keep all your tools well oiled," Doc says.

I polish the bell of the horn with a soft cloth.

"Girls like a clean and shiny horn."

I won't laugh at any of his jokes.

"What's the agenda, man?"

"Yeah, all right," Doc says.

We're going out for some softshell crab and Turbo Dogs at a little Creole joint on Louisiana Avenue, then to the Uptown Cigar Bar on Tchoupitoulas where I'm playing with a trio, The Three Folkers, something like Leadbelly's "Goodnight, Irene," I guess, that kind of basic red beans and rice blues, and later about midnight trucking on over to Maple Leaf Bar on Oak Street, where the place will be hopping, all the tightassed college kids, to the Papa Funk Circus, and there I'm the guest funk horn player.

"Yeah, all right," I say.

"You love these guys," Doc says.

"All right."

I pack up my horn, snapping the clips on the case, and

set it down on the floor by the outside door. My heart and soul are in that case. I think about that last sentence, eight words: *My heart and soul are in that case,* and a little wave of icy crystals passes like loneliness through my whole body, and I shiver as if thrown into a freezer.

"Christ," I say.

I clap my hands together hard, again, and a third time. Doc hands me another glass with a couple shots neat of Wild Turkey, and I swallow half of it in one gulp.

"Hey, these guys, you too, love," Doc says.

"All right," I say.

"One note, you always drive people crazy."

"I know that."

"Sweet horn."

"Okay, shut up."

"What's got you so fucking uptight?"

"You shot a man dead this morning."

"Oh, man, that, that's bothering you, that?"

"Yes."

"Look, this is New Orleans," Doc says. "Things work different here."

"You can't just shoot people."

"People get shot every day."

"But what about the cops?"

Doc shrugs.

"What can they do," he says, "take away my constitutional rights?"

Doc laughs.

He pours himself another double.

"More?"

"All right," I say.

Doc pours Wild Turkey into my glass and we clink our glasses together.

"Cheers."

"All right."

We drink.

"Know what I think will happen?" Doc says.

"Yeah, all right."

"The cops will notify his mama that the workman was trespassing on the job and got what he deserved. Case closed."

"You're kidding."

"Bet you hundred bucks," Doc says.

He holds out his hand. I shake my head. Doc laughs.

"Chickenshit," he says.

"I'm ready to go," said Ms Sugarlicq.

She stood at the top of the stairs, dressed in a black rubber leotard, a silk scarf of bloodred fire binding her long hair tight, a knotted whip of blonde coiling down her long white neck. Bloodred lipstick, red nails, spike heels.

"Where you going, baby?"

"With you."

"No, you're not going with us."

"Yes, I am."

"Honey, Doc and I made other plans."

"Change your plans."

She descended the stairs, fell to her knees and crawled across the floor to my crotch, lunging with her twisting mouth to try to grab hold of my cock with her teeth through the fabric of my pants.

I let her nuzzle and bite.

I pushed her away.

"No, don't," she said.

"Do what you want, baby," I said.

Ms Sugarlicq got up on her feet, up on her spike heels.

She was a good three inches taller than me.

"You're not doing it with me," I said.

"I'll fuck the first man I see," she said.

Ms Sugar opened the front door. The yellow outside light was on, still light out, the insects circling in a lavender sweat of early evening heat.

"Use rubbers," I said.

"Fuck you."

Ms S was wobbling, but she stepped out the door.

"I'll suck them raw."

The door slammed shut.

"God damn her," I said.

I opened the door and stepped outside. Ms Sugarlicq was trying to run away down the broken rubble banquette.

She turned around.

"Fuck you," she said.

She screamed.

"Fuck you."

She turned down the banquette again and stumbled ahead a couple of steps, falling down to hands and knees. Coming up behind, I grabbed her around the waist and pulled her to her feet.

She tried to slap me away, but I was stronger and had my hands and arms around her body. I wasn't going to let go of her, and she struggled against me, trying to knee me in the crotch and step on my feet with her spikes, but I got both her hands behind her back, holding both wrists with my left hand and gripping her by the neck with my right thumb and index finger.

"Let go of me," she said.

"You're coming with me," I said.

I led her ahead of me, keeping a firm grip on her crossed wrists and the nape of her neck, to the metal toolshed where Doc Nawlins kept the bicycles locked up. In order to open the door, I had to let go of her neck, and she struggled and kicked against me, finally breaking free by stepping through the open door into the toolshed. She grabbed up a shovel and turned around, aiming the curved edge of the blade at my crotch, and charged.

I stepped aside, grabbing onto the shovel handle with both hands and wrestled it free of her grip. I spun her around and pinned her hard with a high stick against the toolshed door, knocking the wind out of her. Once more, I had her wrists together behind her back.

I grabbed a roll of duct tape and wrapped it several turns around her crossed wrists. Next, I bound her ankles with duct tape and finally put a stop to the screaming with a swatch of tape across her pretty red mouth. I put her down between the two bicycles.

"Sorry, Ms Sugar, but you're staying in tonight."

I closed the toolshed door and locked it with the padlock.

That was the end to that.

For now.

"Fuck."

Already she was kicking the door.

All Night Long

We go to the restaurant. Doc Nawlins has his girlfriend, Judy Tubes, a big-titted girl from Atlanta, Georgia, wearing a size too tight hot pants, but ask if my eyes are complaining, I'd have to say no. I get the softshell crab. Doc wants crawfish etouffée, and Judy orders the blackened catfish.

When the waiter goes back into the kitchen, Judy looks around the room. We're the only customers in the restaurant.

"Bet I could give both you guys handjobs before he gets back," Judy says.

"Fifty bucks," Doc says.

He throws a folded bill on the table.

"Sorry, Judy," I say, shrugging sheepishly. "I have to play tonight."

Doc unzips his pants, and Judy goes to work.

Here comes the waiter with my softshell crab, roasted potatoes, a side salad of tomato, lettuce and sweet onion in a basil vinaigrette, and a basket of gigitts.

The waiter sniffs.

Doc coughs.

"I'll need another napkin," Doc says.

"You right," the waiter says.

Judy picks up the folded bill and sticks it between her tits.

The softshell crab is delicious.

We go to the Uptown Cigar Bar.

The Three Folkers are two guitars and a standup bass.

Three good players.

I sit in through the whole second set, finishing off with "Goodnight, Irene."

These boys are nice to me.

Playing the sweet lyric, I feel kind of sad about Ms Sugarlicq bound and gagged in the toolshed, kind of sad about what a mean bastard I can be sometimes . . . oh my . . .

" . . . I'll see you in my dreams . . . "

The horn is sweet. I always have a sweet horn, and the crowd in the small bar gives me a warm welcome. Lots of college girls smoking cigars and drinking Jack Daniels. They won't let me buy a drink.

Doc Nawlins and Judy Tubes have a small table in the middle of the room. Judy has her hand on Doc's crotch. He has a hand on hers. They're both smoking cigars.

"Going out for some air," I say.

Outside on the banquette in front of the bar, Tchoupitoulas Street is completely deserted. I could be standing in the middle of a ghost town. Blocks away, a siren approaches like rising static.

"Hey, Lewis."

Emerging from the darkness across the street, a man on a wobbly bicycle is waving furiously and calling my name.

"Lewis," he says.

It's the friend of mine that I keep having dreams about.

"Paul?" I say.

What the hell is he doing in New Orleans?

He turns the bicycle to cross the street and is struck immediately by the oncoming ambulance.

"Watch out," I say.

The ambulance impales the bicycle, throwing Paul into the air, and squeals to a stop in the middle of the street. Paul bounces across the pavement and hits his head hard. Like someone has turned on a tap, a puddle of dark blood begins to spread beneath his blue bicycle helmet.

Two medics with a stretcher leap from the back doors of the ambulance.

I step into the street.

"Stay back," a medic says.

"Friend of mine," I say.

"Back," he says.

I step back onto the banquette.

The two medics put Paul on the stretcher. They put the stretcher and the crumpled bicycle in the ambulance, get in and close the doors behind them.

Lights flash. The siren wails.

The ambulance drives away.

I walk into the empty street. The pool of blood that spilled from his head like wine from a broken bottle has disappeared, and when I crouch down to touch the spot, the pavement is dry and hard as bone. Where did all the blood go? The medics didn't mop it up.

It's as if nothing has happened.

Am I dreaming again?

A horn blares, and a speeding car passes closely, missing me by inches.

I shake my fist at the taillights.

"Asshole," I say.

Someone puts a hand on my shoulder.

"You okay?" Doc says.

My hands are trembling, *my head buzzing with a sound like a downed wire in a rain puddle.*

"Did you see that?" I say.

"Drunk in a hurry, I reckon, to get to the next drive-in daiquiri stand," Doc says.

"No, the ambulance hit that guy."

"What guy?"

"Friend of mine from back home."

"Here?"

"Yes."

Doc looks down at the anonymous, innocent pavement of the street. He shrugs.

"You ready go?" he says.

"Yeah, you right."

We drive uptown via St Charles Avenue through the oak trees and Spanish moss of Audubon Park and into Carrollton. If Doc Nawlins misses a pothole in the road between Tchoupitoulas and Oak Street, I don't know which one.

I'm curled up, a burned-out, middle-aged fetus in the back seat, clutching my trumpet case like a doll.

Judy Tubes leans over the back of the front seat.

"I like to be spanked," she says.

My hands are still trembling and beat on the trumpet case like a drum.

"Why don't you spank me real soon?" she says.

"There's a strap in the glove compartment," Doc says.

Judy hisses a wicked laugh.

"I'll be bad for you," she says.

"Okay."

Doc finds a parking space across the street from the Maple Leaf Bar.

Doc gets out.

"I'll find a table in the garden," he says.

Doc walks away, and Judy crawls into the back seat with the leather strap in her hand.

She pulls down her hot pants. She's not wearing panties. On her left bum cheek, there's a tattoo of a rattlesnake ready to strike.

She hands me the strap.

"Unzip your fly," she says.

She puts her hands in my pants, and my cock swells to her touch.

"Spank me," she says.

She leans down into my crotch and circles the cap of my cock with her tongue. Her bare ass is two half moons in the rear window. There's barely enough room for us to move around, but I raise my hand and bring the strap down on the head of the rattlesnake.

Judy flinches.

She nibbles the teardrop lip of flesh at the base of my cock.

"Harder than that," she says.

She licks my cock like an ice cream cone.

I bring the strap down, harder this time, and a line of pink welt like an eraser's trail runs through the rattle on the snake's tail.

Judy flinches.

She deep throats my cock like a fish swallowing a fish.

"Harder," she says.

She chokes and comes up for breath.

"Please," she says.

I bring the strap down.

She pumps my cock with her hand.

"Yes."

I bring the strap down.

"Yes."

Judy pumps my throbbing cock.

I bring the strap down.

"Yes."

The pink welts spread like crosshatching. Judy pumps, and I begin to come.

I bring the strap down, harder this time.

Judy puts her mouth around my cock, her lips tight and pursed, and my come floods into the back of her throat.

"Oh, my god," I say.

I drop the strap and it clumps on the floor of the back seat.

The windows of the car are opaque with our heavy breathing.

"Thank you," Judy says.

We get out of the car.

"I have to play now."

We walk across the street to the bar and I grip the handle of the trumpet case as if holding onto a branch while hanging over a precipice.

The Maple Leaf Bar is a ruined beauty with sixteen foot ceilings and a paneled, maple wood bar that runs forty feet to the back of the front room. Behind the bar is an oak-framed full-length mirror behind liquor bottle shelves as high as a person standing on a stool on tiptoe can reach, and above the mirror is an enormous oil painting of an odalisque with a mischievous grin, bidding one and all to drink and be merry from her naked, precariously-angled perch on a paisley-patterned, velvet chaise longue. With her hands behind her neck, the only discretion to her pose is the careful placement of a red rosebud between her crossed, milkwhite legs.

The second room in the bar, a large dancehall, is the home of backbeat funk, and the funk band Papa Funk Circus is funking it up at centre stage for their hip and funky fans. Papa Funk is three guitars, two full drumkits, plus bongos, standup bass, electric piano, and a red plastic electric sax. They put out a pulsing, repetitive, hot, crazy gumbo beat of backbeat bass and primitive drum rhythms, plus lots of bright and sexy sax and piano riffs, big chunks of electric ivory, all of it to get you up and out of your old rocking chair for some time to come.

The room is packed, everybody dancing individually, facing the stage with the band for their partner, and Judy and I have to fight our way through the young college crowd to the back door which is wide open to a verdant jungle patio garden where birds sing in the green trees, and mint juleps are two for one. Doc has a glasstop table in the corner and waves us over.

"So what did you two get up to?" Doc says.

"No good," I say.

Judy laughs her wicked laugh.

"I don't think I can play here tonight," I say.

"What the hell is this?" Doc says.

"I'm fucked up."

"You're getting paid to play."

"Yeah, you right."

"Damn right."

A waiter drops three bottles of Abita Red on the table. Doc waves away my ten dollar bill and pays for the round. I drink my beer in one gulp, slamming the empty bottle down on the table top.

"Careful," Doc says.

I stand up and lean down with my arms spread and my hands down with splayed fingers on the table.

"Sometimes you want to bang a bottle down so hard on a table that it breaks at the base and slices your hand in two," I say.

My hands are turning blue.

"What the hell are you talking about?" Doc says.

"Where's the restroom?"

"Back through the crowd."

I take my hands off the table, and their ghostly outlines on the glass top slowly fade.

"Watch my trumpet."

The men's restroom is not much larger than a phone booth, and it's packed shoulder to shoulder. Every step you have to be careful not to step on somebody's shoes. Finally, I'm next in line at the urinal. The guy in front of me has a bunch of T-shirts thrown over his right shoulder. He pulls down the flush handle and turns around, zipping up his pants.

"Paul," I say.

"Hi, Lewis," he says.

"What the hell are you doing here?"

"Selling Lewis King T-shirts."

"I saw you run down in the street."

"Look."

Paul unfurls one of the T-shirts. On the front, there's a black and white photo of me playing my horn two hours ago at The Cigar Bar, and below that, in Old English script, are the words *Lewis 'Sweet Horn' King.*

"I'm your number one fan," Paul says.

The guy behind me pushes against my back.

"Hey, pal, you pissing or what?" he says.

I step away from the urinal.

"Take it."

Paul pushes his way toward the door.

"Paul."

"Guy wants to buy one of these," he says.

"Talk to me, man."

The restroom door opens. The roaring surge of the backbeat funk rushes in, and Paul is swallowed by the swelling crowd.

I look for him all around the bar, squeezing my way through the sweet, nubile crush, the hot funky beat of the dance floor, swelling with spontaneous desire, brushing anonymous breasts and shoulders, firm butts, soft thighs, trading sweat for an exchange of flashing, leering eyes, the emotional moment naked to the promise of sweetly-rotten oblivion, sex without condition, sex without identity, sex without sex, but there's no one selling T-shirts, no sign of Paul.

I walk outside, look up and down the street.

Getting down on my hands and knees, I bark like a dog.

"Lewis."

I turn around.

Doc Nawlins is standing in the doorway of the bar.

"Lewis," he says.

I lick the pavement of the street, and it tastes like tar, congealed hog belly fat, and beer vomit.

"Yeah?"

"Papa Funk is looking for you."

I get up on my feet, wobbling. I reach out for something vertical to hold on to, but like Paul, there's nothing there, and I fall down into the street again.

There's an image in my mind the next day: I'm playing funk trumpet with the Papa Funk Circus, and I'm sweet, my horn is always sweet, and the college girls go wild and buy me drinks.

"You going to play?" Doc says.

"Yeah, you right."

Staggering up Doc Nawlins's driveway, I fall down and crawl on all fours to the toolshed.

I fumble with the key in the padlock.

"Give me a hand here."

Doc takes the key and unlocks the toolshed door. One whole side of the aluminum toolshed has been kicked out, and there's a gummy residue of duct tape stuck to the links of one of the bicycle chains. Ms Sugarlicq is gone.

"My fucking shed," Doc says.

I run down the street.

"Lewis."

I keep running. The night is hot. I'm hot. Sweat swells and pours over me like hot water from an open tap. I run beneath the oak trees, running in the impersonal, wearing heat, the darkest hour of my life, and I run into Ms Sugarlicq, staggering barefoot out of the dark down the broken rubble of the banquette. Remnants of duct tape are still wrapped around the wrists of her black rubber jumpsuit, and they trail behind like gummy flags of freedom from her black rubber ankles. The swatch of duct tape that I put over her mouth is now fastened like a crude bandage across her forehead. Her lower lip is swollen purple, and a trickle of dark blood runs down the curve of her chin. We hug each other close, as close as two people can get without crawling inside each other, and kiss deeply.

"I love you," she says.

"I love you, too."

"I've been bad," she says.

She smells like cigarettes and sex and violence and camellias.

"I've been bad too, baby."

"Spank me," she says.

The Naked and The Dead

Waking up naked on the kitchen floor, my back is all sticky. I've been sleeping in spilled beer, and pulling myself off the floor is like tearing velcro. I try to sit up, but it makes my head hurt, and I fall back to the floor into the sticky spill. There's a half bottle of Abita Red within reach of my left hand, and reaching out for it I tip it over and flat beer spills across the floor. I sit up, pick up the bottle and put it to my mouth. I swallow the warm beer and a cigarette butt which I spit out, but it sticks like a dead bug to my right thigh. I brush the soggy butt away and it shits a line of wet black ash down my leg. I get up on my feet, gag and cough and stagger, bouncing against the fridge and into the door of the closet-sized bathroom beside the washer and dryer. I fall to my knees and try to throw up into the toilet but can't and only gag and spit and dry heave. I get up and stumble against the sink, turning on the cold water tap. I throw water with my hands against my face and over the top of my head. I do this again and again until my brain feels cold and I'm no longer too proud to look in the mirror.

Oh my god.

Back in the kitchen, I open the fridge door and look inside for a long time. The stale cold feels good to me, and the little lightbulb is reassuring. Three kinds of beer. I knock one over. I pick it up. I open the beer, guzzling it down. I get another one and guzzle half of it.

I feel a little better and close the fridge door.

Where the hell are my clothes?

Ms Sugarlicq in jetblack silk pjs sleeps curled up on the couch in the living room. I try to kiss her, but she flicks her hand above her mouth like swatting a fly, and I pull away. I lie down on the rug below the couch and try to hold her hand, but she rolls away. I fall asleep. Paul is lying on the couch, naked from the waist down, wearing a 'Lewis King' T-shirt splattered with dried blood. His face is caved in like a broken coconut. Sticky blood everywhere. I'm holding his cold, clammy hand.

I sit up.

The couch is bare.

Ms Sugar's legs going up the stairs.

"Pig," she says.

On hands and knees, I follow her up the stairs. I stagger into the bedroom, leaning against the doorway to keep from falling down. Ms Sugar is lying on top of the covers on the bed, pretending to sleep.

"What the hell you just call me?"

I fall on the bed and bounce against her.

Ms Sugar gets up.

"You smell like shit," she says.

"Come back to bed."

"Like pigshit."

She grabs up some jogging shorts, a little top and her running shoes, and is out the door. I can hear her going down the stairs. I stagger to the doorway. She's changing her clothes in front of the front door. She slips into some panties and puts her jogging shorts on. She puts on her runners, squatting to tie them up. Last, she puts on her top.

"Come on, baby," I say.

Ms Sugarlicq lifts her head up and screams.

"PIGSHIT!"

She goes out the door and slams it shut.

Doc Nawlins storms out of his bedroom.

"What the hell is your girlfriend . . . fuck, man, you smell like death or something," he says.

"Do I?"

"God damn, Lewis, go take a shower."

He retreats to his bedroom.

"I'm going to gag," he says.

He closes the bedroom door. I can hear him gagging on the other side.

A Streetcar Named Charles

At the neutral ground stop on Hilary Street, we run to catch the vintage electric streetcar, almost full, grabbing seats across the aisle from each other on the hard oak and brass benches, laughing and breathing, sharing a bag of Zapps sweet potato chips. Open windows, cooling breeze, the streetcar races the high, lazy clouds drifting parallel to the tracks and the overhead wires along St Charles Avenue.

Shade and sun. Audubon Park strollers. Gated oaks and Spanish moss. Palms, porticoes, white wicker weather. Southern mansions set like jewels in finely spun lawns of green gold.

Brakes squeal.

Clang, clang.

The streetcar driver, a lean, no-nonsense woman about forty, makes no doubt who runs this show.

"Move to the back, please."

Standing room only.

Clang, clang.

"You have to wait."

I give up my seat to a woman with shopping bags and two small children.

"Move back."

Ms Sugar waves bye-bye as I shuffle towards the back of the streetcar. A ten-year-old boy in a freshly-pressed white shirt slowly and patiently moves against the flow, squeezing around everybody in the crowded aisle.

"Excuse me," he says.

He makes it all the way to the front of the streetcar, twisting, ducking, squeezing by, and turns around to come all the way back again.

Clang, clang.

"Excuse me," he says.

A woman laughs at him.

"Why did you come back?"

"I don't know."

"You little rascal."

In the swing and slow sway of the streetcar, the hot day burning steel and jasmine flower, The Big Easy goes down slow. Portico after portico along the cracked concrete banquette parades past the open windows. Front porches, shirt sleeves, mint juleps. A pink-column mansion rots like a giant peach in the sun. A Turkish rug takes all day to hang from a wrought iron balcony.

The oak trees along the avenue are a grand and elegant gesture. Street level, neutral ground tree branches reach, snap, slapping green through the open windows.

The streetcar is hot and sweet. The buzzer insists like a dentist's drill. The streetcar motor beats like a drum in cardiac arrest. The streetcar wheels grind, kissing the tracks *like a tearing of endless silk.*

Ms Sugarlicq has moved, and I don't know where she is, just hope she's still aboard. At the moment I'm more interested in the young woman with carrot-rasta hair, wearing thick wire jewelry and a dainty black lace top, who stands close in front and keeps pushing her body into mine.

Her bare arms and naked back covered in voodoo tombstone tattoos, she pushes even harder when my thick hard-on rams into her from behind when the car suddenly stops.

Voodoo queen or Tulane freshman?

The lazy sun sprawls, taking all the space on an empty bench, and the two of us run, hand in hand, for the seat, sitting down side by side. We grab each other by the crotch and hang on. The voodoo freshman has a sketchbook which she opens to dark pages of pen-and-ink oak tree Spanish moss vampire violence. While I leaf through the open sketchbook spread across my lap, she unzips my pants and proceeds to give me head on the streetcar named Charles.

On the bench in front of us, a man with a white beard leans with his arm out an open window to hold up a skyscraper.

Taut strings of city traffic sing at the intersection of Calliope Street and St Charles Avenue.

At Lee Circle, the gentleman general's dignified statue graciously surrenders focus to twin little girls in fuchsia tunics sitting on a stone bench below him.

A rock 'n' roll band atop a truckbed at curbside blooms into rhythm and blues.

Not quite as many police cars as pretty women.

Burned chicory coffee air.

I come in the Tulane freshman voodoo queen's silk-lined mouth.

Clang, clang.

"End of the line."

Zipping my pants. Putting away the sketchbook.

There's Ms Sugar at the front of the streetcar, french kissing a young sailor.

"Get off. End of the line."

The streetcar driver pulls the young sailor off Ms S and shows him the door.

"Get off."

He staggers off the streetcar. Ms S follows right behind, and they resume their french kissing on the banquette.

Vieux Carré

"You're insane."

"You're insane."

"You're insane."

"You're insane."

"You're insane."

"You're insane."

"You're insane."

"You're mad."

"You're mad."

Crossing Canal Street, we're walking New Orleans into the heart of the French Quarter, Vieux Carré, down legendary Bourbon, walking on opposite sides of the fermenting street.

"You're a sour cabbage."

She pulls a tit out of her blouse.

"Come to mama, come to mama," she says.

A blues drummer busker with two sticks and a white plastic pail sprawls across the banquette. I give him a buck.

"Good luck with the sticks, pal."

"Good luck with the ho," he says.

Three boys tap dance in the street, and I give them two dollars. The smallest boy clips me in the ankle.

"I ain't working for them, mister."

"You right. And I ain't working for you."

The two older boys, ten or eleven, swarm Ms Sugar, pinching her ass, grabbing her tits. I make short work of their callow chins with the buttend of my trumpet case, and soon Ms Sugar and I are walking down the street again.

She shakes off my hold on her arm.

"I don't need your help."

"You need all the help you can get, baby."

"Let's go in here," she says.

She walks into a fetish shop, right past the free demonstration of a battery-operated dildo and goes straight up the studded rubber stairs to the second floor.

I follow behind.

The second floor is a livery stable warehouse of leather leashes, straps, harnesses, belts and collars, whips, ropes, blindfolds, red silk, black lace, ball bats, rubber clothing, studs and metal rings.

"Let's dress you like a baby," she says.

"I'm not a baby."

"You like titty."

"I like it all."

"I know, a little boy," she says.

"No."

"A boy who likes it all."

"No."

"A schoolgirl, then."

"No."

"Yes."

And so I dress up like a Catholic schoolgirl, white starched blouse, red tie, navy blue pleated skirt, kneehigh socks, and black pumps. I put on a beautiful Creole wig and look at myself in the full-length mirror. Laughing, sticking out my tongue at the ridiculous costume, I have to be the ugliest schoolgirl in the history of New Orleans who ever sang, "*St Ann, St Ann, send me a man!*"

"What is this laughter?" says Ms Sugarlicq.

She steps out of the dressing room. She wears a nun's habit of the St Ursuline sisters. In her right hand is a black leather riding crop.

"This is stupid," I say.

"Have you been a good girl?"

"Fuck you."

She slaps me across the face with the riding crop. My lower lip splits. I touch it with my fingertips. There's blood. I can taste blood in my mouth.

The nun's habit falls to the floor at Ms Sugarlicq's feet, and she is now dressed as a dominatrix in plunging black leather and red satin, shoulder pads, knee pads, spike heels, black lace stockings and red-ribboned garters. Stepping forward out of the fallen habit, she slaps the riding crop across her knee pad.

Snap.

"Have you been a good girl?" she says.

"This is bullshit."

She raises the riding crop, readying to strike again.

"Don't hit me."

We stare at each other.

I won't smile.

I won't break.

I won't give in on this.

I won't play her games.

But her stare is fixed and hard as ice, the dense, heavy stare of an alien from a planet where cruelty is as strong as the law of gravity.

For a moment, I look away.

She smiles sweetly.

I smile, too.

"Okay?"

"Kiss my feet," she says.

"Yeah right."

Mockingly, I get down on my knees, put my hands on the floor and obsequiously lean forward to kiss the polished toe of her leather boot. Ms S slips a black leather dog collar and harness around my neck, raises my skirt with the looping tip of the riding crop and slaps my ass hard.

Snap.

Pain like a knife of fire slices through my body, cutting across my feverish brain, and I begin to cry.

"Don't hurt me, please, don't hurt me."

On the black rubber rug at the foot of the till on the second floor of the fetish shop, I roll up into a ball and cry like a baby.

"Mommy doesn't want to hurt."

Ms Sugarlicq beats me black and blue with the riding crop, and the sexy sales clerk behind the counter rolls her eyes and rings up a sale.

"Oh, no, Mommy doesn't want to hurt."

Back down on Bourbon Street, electric blues, rhythm and blues, and Dixieland jazz boom live out of three consecutive bars. A mule-and-carriage races by at a trot. A stripper shimmies in a window. A barker in a shiny suit has a card that reads: *three drinks for one.* His partner tap dances on a hard board.

Sin City.

"Y'all come here."

Postcards, voodoo, T-shirts, slurpies, three thousand varieties of hot sauce. Burlap bags swollen wet with oysters lean in a doorway. A garbage truck stalls. Hanging out a limousine window, a white poodle puppy poses for a picture. All the beautiful babes in New Orleans. People walk down the street with drinks in their hands. They laugh. They dance. They fall down and throw up on the banquette.

Beneath the crumbling plaster of the cupola in the 18th-century courtyard garden at Napoleon House, big potted plants shade our afternoon table from the hot sun. Surrounded by the smells of rotting antiquity and Creole cooking, the efficient, no-nonsense waiter brings us French bread and soft butter and hot sauce. After a good beating, I'm always cleansed, exhausted and famished. We each order a muffeletta, jambalaya, insalata, and a seafood gumbo. A party at the next table gives us a plate of crab cakes, saying they ordered too much, and we take it eagerly.

Built for Napoleon by an admirer, the ex-emperor died of arsenic poisoning before he could escape his final exile and reconnoiter to New Orleans for a third coming and the gift of this house. Dr Antommarchi, his personal physician on St Helena, the one who administered the arsenic, later practised medicine in New Orleans for thirteen years while living at this address.

"The physician heals himself," I say.

"It doesn't get any better than this," Ms Sugar says.

We drink from frosted bottles of Abita Red. We poke the tines of our forks into a shared, hot bowl of bread pudding. We smoke cigarettes. We stare lazily into each other's eyes.

"I love you, baby."

"I love you, too."

A busboy passes by, balancing overhead a round tray pre-cariously piled to the sky with dirty dishes. He's wearing a Lewis King T-shirt.

"Hey you."

The boy looks at me, trips over his feet, and the dirty

crockery slides off the edge of the tray and shatters to the floor of the courtyard, breaking into more shards than Napoleon Bonaparte had latent dreams of empire. The boy turns, dropping the empty tray, and runs out of the courtyard into the dark bar.

I get up and run after him.

The boy squeezes around a fat man in the door of the bar and disappears around the corner of Chartres Street.

I run into the arms of the fat man and bounce away. I fight my way around him to the sunlight in the doorway, and it's like fighting against a pillow for air.

"Out of my way."

In the street, a mule pulling a whitewashed cart trots by. The busboy is hanging onto the back by his fingertips.

"Hey."

Chasing after the cart, I run down the middle of the sun-struck street, yelling and waving my arms, but when the mule makes a sharp turn lakeside up Toulouse Street, I stop running. I lean down with my hands on my knees and dry heave. *And down the long unshaded street a vendor of colored ices beats a rainbow of tin bells.* I shouldn't have had that cigarette.

I walk back to Napoleon House and into the courtyard where two boys in white smocks are sweeping up the broken dishes. Ms Sugarlicq is gone. In the middle of the bread pudding remains, a lipstick-stained cigarette butt is impaled like a tumor into a lung. There's a short note scrawled in lipstick on my trumpet case: FUK YU.

"Your check," the waiter says.

He hands me the check.

"Yeah right."

> "... I want to be in that number
> When the saints go marching in ..."

Blowing their hearts out through old brass and threadbare catgut, the street musicians, like birds on a wire, line the hard green benches on the slate banquette in front of sun-washed St Louis Cathedral. Fortune tellers at cardboard card tables flip their garish-coloured cards of fate. The Fool. The Hanged Man. Three swords plunged into a bleeding heart.

Across the paving stone courtyard is the old parade ground Jackson Square, a Louis XIV green grass diamond cut from the sun, and another block away, looking into the sharp light, you can see the levee and the watery brown muscle of the Mississippi River flashing by in the broiling heat.

"Get your ice," the iceman cries.

Looking around for Ms Sugar, I wander Jackson Square, verdant with magnolia, petunia, azalea, fern, purple dawn, Louisiana peppermint camellia, smelling my way to the centre of the parterre where Old Hickory himself, frozen in bronzed violence, rears back on the hind legs of his steed, tips his hat to the sky and charges into history. I sit at the base of his statue and weep like a child abandoned on the street.

Getting up, I stumble forward riverside, crossing Decatur Street, the "Ladies in Red" streetcar tracks, and the Illinois Central railway tracks, finally sitting down again on a bench at Moon Walk Park overlooking the river. The Mississippi is muddy and wide, and it smells like shit, three thousand miles of pure toilet bowl shit, and I have to hang my head to keep from gagging.

"Hi."

It's Ms Sugarlicq.

"Kiss me," she says.

She climbs upon my lap with her legs behind my back and slips her sweet tongue like a buttery flame of roux into my open mouth.

"Welcome to New Orleans."

The tongue slips out of my mouth, and we look up. A big man dressed in rags stands as close to the bench as he can without touching us.

"I is David E. Bone," he says. "I hails from Hazelhurst, Mississippi, and I is a poet."

"What's the 'E' stand for?" I say.

"'Rection."

"Yeah, right."

"I have a poem for lovers," he says.

"I bet."

"Let's hear it," says Ms Sugar.

David E. Bone pulls a wadded ball of interlined exercise paper from his pants pocket, spreads it out between his ham fists, clears his throat with a small *cough, cough,* and recites:

Rose is red, violet is blue,
You is the rose in my heart,
You is the violet in my throat,
You is the biscuit in my roux.

River is brown, sky is gray,
You is the tear in my eye,
You is the bug in my ear,
You is the sugar on my beignet.

You is the locket,
I is the rocket.
Why did you leave me?
Why did you go away?

The one you love, kiss first,
Kiss to kill your thirst,

Kiss until it hurts,
Kiss until your lips do burst!

Oh hey,
Oh yeah,
You right,
You bet.

But if you likes this little verse,
Open please your ample purse,
Or kiss my andouille,
Yours truly.

I is David E. Bone,
On the streets without a home,
The writer of this poetry,
David E. Bone, yours truly.

David E. Bone bows as elegantly as Duke Ellington would at Carnegie Hall, and Ms Sugar falls to her knees before him, clasping her arms tightly around his tree stump legs at the knees.

"I want to give you a blowjob," she says, and nuzzles his crotch.

"You right," says David E. Bone.

I shove a buck in his face.

"Beat it, buddy," I say.

He waves the buck away.

"I wants the lady blowjob," he says.

He drags Ms S over the edge of the levee.

I jump on his back and hammer the sides of his head with my fists.

Bone throws me off, pulls out a homemade knife.

"Shiv you," he says.

I back away with my hands in the air.

"For christ's sake, Lewis," says Ms Sugarlicq.

Her eyes slice mine like knives.

"We're consenting adults," she says.

"You right," says David E. Bone.

"Come here," she says.

Ms Sugar takes him by the hand and leads him over the edge of the levee.

I sit on the bench, smoking a cigarette.

I watch the ferry cross the river to Algiers.

Shit floats, and so does commerce and oil tankers and barges and tugboats and paddle wheelers loaded to the gunwales with one-armed bandits.

"Oh, honey," says a voice in the wind.

The Algiers ferry whistle blows.

I walk away, and the fiery butt of my cigarette bounces once across the banquette before blowing away.

Life floats like shit down the endless river.

A Piece of Pie

I strode resolutely across town, thankful that I was still alive. In the open air outside the French Market, a jazz quintet was playing old-fashioned bebop . . . "*salt peanuts, salt peanuts*" . . . and at a nearby table, a woman was cutting pies into sixths with a knife.

She cut pie after pie.

"What's going on?" I say.

The woman laughs.

"You want a piece of pie?" she says.

"I don't know," I say.

"Peach or apple?"

"Maybe."

"Pecan or coconut?"

"Well."

"Banana cream or French custard?"

"Hmm."

"Sweet potato or Cajun tomato?"

"Oh, really?"

"Or a nice meat pie?"

"What kind?"

"Got rabbit or gator."

"Alligator?"

"It's got a bite."

"Think I'll pass."

"Where you from?"

"Canada."

"Canada?"

"Yeah."

"I thought all you boys from Canada like pie."

"I guess we do."

"Something special then?"

She winks.

"Okay."

"Follow me," she says.

"Yeah right."

She turns around and disappears behind the flap of a black canvas tent. I look around. Other women down the line, like endless reflections in a series of mirrors, are cutting pies into sixths with knives, and all of them are smiling at me. I smile back, part the tent flap and duck under.

It's dark inside the tent, so dark I have to touch myself to know I'm here. Turning around to go back out, I'm disoriented and can't find the flap that let me in. I hear giggling, first to the left, and then to the right.

"Where are you?" I say.

I take a step forward, and splash, I'm standing in water or some kind of liquid like water up to my knees. I hear another more distant giggle, almost an echo like a dull cry over water, and then a heavy, slithering splash. I turn around in the dark, stirring the dark waters. Something like a scaly muscle, hard as oak, pliant, strong and rough as hemp rope, like a long tail, wraps around my ankles and throws me facefirst, splashing into the unseen water. I swallow deeply, choking and thrashing about, my mouth and my throat and my stomach and my lungs drinking, filling with black liquid. I'm hit from behind, a hard blow to the back of my head as if struck by a brick or a dense, water-logged chunk of wood, and a light like white lightning flashes in my eyes and spreads a condensed, raging fire across my brain. My face, lips, teeth and tongue are plunged deeply into the sweetest pussy I've ever tasted, the labia creamy and sweet as camellia blossoms rotting in the rain, and the vagina is wet and hot, its soft flesh vibrating with the deep, persistent beat of a faraway drum. Again the bright light flashes, crackles like tinder igniting, and I'm flying, eyes wide open, through endless space high, high above a pale blue pearl, a lustrous, dull marble on fire from the inside out, which is a sun-glazed image of the round earth, islands of white cloud floating, a blue sea, a blue sky, and consciousness is thrust into the eternal moment of the irredeemable present.

Drowning in Molasses

At the corner of Decatur Street and St Ann on the riverside edge of Jackson Square, across the street from the cast iron, elegant beauty of the Pontalba Apartments built in 1849 by a spoiled brat French baroness who had great taste, I sit alone in the fading sun at an open air table in Café Du Monde with a chicory café au lait and a plate of beignets. A snowy drifting of powdered sugar and cigarette ash down my shirt-front—playing clandestine footsie, when her boyfriend isn't looking, with a young woman at the next table—I watch the passing scene of porkfat tourists padding by in shirtsleeves and sandals. And sketch artists, street musicians, jugglers, clowns, crones, voodoo queens, Creole fortune tellers, hot dog hawkers, ice cream vendors, street cleaners, bums, kids, dogs, mules pulling carts, con men, easy women, hard women, pretty women, and cops. Lots and lots of cops.

"Let go of me."

Ms Sugar, in handcuffs, struggles against the custody of a bareheaded cop maybe all of nineteen years old and sucking on a lollipop.

"I know him."

She points at me and kicks the cop in the shins.

"Ouch. Be nice."

"Lewis."

She drags the cop to my table.

"You responsible for this woman?"

"Nope."

"God damn you, Lewis."

Ms Sugar kicks the table, and my coffee spills across the table top like a river flooding over a break in a levee. I jump up from my chair, knocking it over backwards, and people at the next table scramble out of the way.

"Jesus, bitch."

"Fuck you, Lewis."

"She seems to know you."

"That don't make me responsible for her."

Ms Sugar kicks the cop.

"Will you stop it?"

"No."

The cop looks at her. He looks at me. He sucks on his lollipop, screwing up his face as if trying to use his brains for the first time in his life.

"Hundred bucks, she's yours."

"A hundred dollars?"

"You right, five Andy Jacksons."

"Forget it."

"Ah, man, come on."

A waiter passes by, ignoring the spill at the table.

"Can I get another cup of coffee?"

He walks away.

"Hey, I'm talking to you."

The waiter keeps walking.

The lollipop cop taps me on the shoulder.

"Give me a break," he says.

Ms Sugarlicq hangs her head. She's about to cry.

"I love you," she says.

"Christ."

I pull out my billfold and count my cash.

"Sixty-three bucks is all I got."

"Good enough."

He grabs the money from my hand and begins to walk away.

"Hey."

He turns around.

"Take off the cuffs."

"Yeah right."

Ms Sugar slumps into the chair beside me.

"I do love you," she says.

"Just try keeping your pants on for five minutes."

"Don't be mean."

She's crying.

"Come here, baby."

I put my arm around her.

"I love you, too."

We're nose to nose, and like two bunnies, rub them together. She opens her mouth, and we kiss deeply.

"There's the two lovebirds."

It's Doc Nawlins and Judy Tubes.

"Hiya," says Judy.

"Oh, hi," I say.

She leans down and gives me a big wet kiss on the lips.

"Good to see you again."

"Good to see you, too."

Ms Sugarlicq pinches my arm.

"What's that for?"

"I'm here, too," she says.

"Yeah, right."

I introduce Judy to Ms Sugar.

"Howdy-do," says Judy.

"Hi," says Ms S.

The two women walk around each other like two jittery cats ready to fight.

"Y'all ready now for a French Quarter bar crawl?" says Doc.

"Yeah, right."

The streetlights are on. Yellow walls are now gold, and red walls are fresh blood. The cathedral is a white block of carved salt in a peach sky *deepening to purple over the river*. Crooners stroll through the dark green shade of Jackson Square. The trees sing with dark birds. Fortune tellers bark like dogs, hiss like snakes, *laughing all around us in the dusk*. A marching band passes by out of nowhere . . . "Swing Low, Sweet Chariot" . . . and disappears around a corner of night. Everywhere people are spilling their drinks, puking in the magnolias, wrestling in the middle of the neon streets, and kaleidoscopic New Orleans begins to spin.

We go into O'Flaherty's Pub, drink three or four pints of Irish ale. The owner of the pub drops by our table, and Doc introduces me.

"Heard about your sweet horn," he says, shaking my hand.

"The sweetest," says Judy.

"What would you know?" says Ms S.

"Lots," says Judy.

We go to Felix's Restaurant & Bar for oysters on the half shell with lemon and dynamite Louisiana hot sauce, drink three or four Abita Reds.

Ms Sugarlicq spills her drink in Judy's lap.

"Oh, I'm so sorry," says Ms Sugar.

Topless dancers, strippers, drag queens, B-girls, waiters, bartenders, and the hoarse-voiced doormen barkers. We go into Lafitte's Blacksmith Shop for an open container mint julep.

"Quadruples," says Doc.

"You right," says the bartender.

It's a tradition. In this bar in 1814, Andrew Jackson and the pirate Jean Lafitte were drinking quadruple mint juleps while plotting together the Battle of New Orleans.

Judy spills her drink over Ms Sugar's head.

"Oh, my," says Judy.

We wander down Bourbon Street with drinks in hand. Mine is a good quart of bourbon, mint leaves and ice. Mostly bourbon.

"I love to sin," Doc says.

"Yeah right."

Judy and Ms Sugar keep throwing hip checks into each other.

"Girls," says Doc, "if you don't behave I'm going tie you both up in bags and hang you from a street lamp."

"Fuck you," say the women.

We stumble in the dark down Orleans Street behind St Louis Cathedral past Tennessee Williams's second-floor apartment where he wrote *Vieux Carré*. And just around the corner from the gigantic backlit shadow of "Touchdown Jesus" against the white wall of the cathedral, is William Faulkner's balcony apartment where he penned the novel *A Soldier's Pay*.

"Who gives a shit about that shit?" says Ms Sugar.

She's having trouble standing up.

"People with class," says Judy.

"Class my ass," says Ms Sugar.

She sucker punches Judy with a short right to the chin. Judy falls down on the banquette, pulling Ms S down on top of her. The two women wrestle, rolling into the street. They pull each other's hair. A small crowd begins to gather around them.

"I love a cat fight," says Doc.

Emerging from the crowd, the lollipop cop and a Creole fortune teller jump into the fray to pull the two women apart. Ms Sugarlicq kicks the lollipop cop in the shins. He hops about, pulls his revolver and fires it into the air.

Everybody freezes.

Blue smoke drifts with the smell of cordite in the street. The only sound is someone puking a block away.

"How's your momma and dem?" says the cop.

He handcuffs Ms S and Judy together.

"A hundred dollars apiece for these women," he says.

"Lewis?" says Ms Sugar.

"Fuck, baby, you know I don't have it."

"Fifty bucks then," says the cop.

"Oh, hell, take them away," says Doc. "They're nothing but trouble."

I step into the street.

"Why don't you just let them go?"

"Freeze."

The lollipop cop points his revolver pointblank at my chest. I freeze alright, then very slowly raise my arms into the air.

But I can't stop talking.

"The fight's over anyway."

"Son of a bitch," the cop says.

He takes a step closer.

"On your fucking knees," he says.

I hesitate.

"Do I have to kill you, fuck?"

I get down on my knees.

He takes a step closer and puts the nose of the revolver hard against the back of my head behind my right ear.

I look up and make eye contact.

"Please don't shoot me."

Someone on a bicycle falls down in the street right behind the lollipop cop.

It's Paul.

The cop spins around and shoots Paul pointblank in the head. Paul staggers to his feet. He's got half his head blown away, holding his jaw in his hands, but he's on his feet, and with half a mouth he tries to speak.

"Catch me if you can," he says.

Paul turns and runs down the banquette, disappearing around the corner of Pirate's Alley. The cop drops his revolver, and it clatters on the pavement. His lollipop pops out of his mouth, and he faints dead away, dropping to the street like a shot hog.

I get to my feet and run after Paul.

Rounding the corner at Pirate's Alley, someone sticks out a foot and trips me, and I fly headfirst into darkness.

"Shiv you, fuck."

It's David E. Bone, and he slashes out his right arm, a searing flash, and a deep, wet burn like a spilling of hot coals slices through my belly. I'm holding strings of fat sausages stuffed with hot, stewing shit in my hands. Hot strings of sausages pump out of my belly like I'm a sausage machine. I can't hold them all in my hands, they spill over, pumping, a foul, coarse stooling of fetid shit and blood and sausages coiling over my shoes up to my pant cuffs, soaking wet with soggy shit sausages, and here come my blackened lungs, and my heart follows, falling out at my feet, and I chase it across the banquette, bouncing willy nilly like a slimy football in and out of my arms.

"Lewis."

Doc is shaking me.

I look around. I'm sitting on the pavement against the curb where the lollipop cop put the gun to my head. I put my hand on my stomach. The middle button on my shirt has popped off, but I'm not cut. I'm whole, absolutely intact, and I can hear the ocean roar of my beating heart exactly where it's supposed to be.

My trumpet case is beside me, and I pick it up, hugging it close to my chest like a lover.

Slowly I get to my feet.

I feel like shit.

"Come here, Lewis," Doc says.

He's standing across the street with a big, tall woman in a scarlet dress.

"I want you to meet somebody."

For some reason, I'm turning around and around, trying to use the trumpet case for ballast and balance.

I stop.

I'm wobbly on my knees.

"Where's Ms Sugar?"

"Both the chippies went off with the cop."

"Arrested?"

"Arm in arm in arm to the first cockroach hotel room, I reckon."

"Where's the bicycle?"

"At home."

"My friend Paul, the cop shot him in the head?"

"Stop talking shit, Lewis."

"You right."

I walk across the street.

"Lewis, I want you to meet the greatest actress who's ever lived in New Orleans," Doc says.

The big woman laughs. The filtered end of her cigarette is slathered in scarlet lipstick.

"Doc always wants to polish my shoes," she says to me.

"Ms Desirée Eternité," says Doc, and he bows.

"Pleased to meet you, ma'am."

I offer a feeble handshake, and she takes my hand carefully like a wounded, orphan bird between her soft and tender, compassionate hands.

"Living in New Orleans is like drowning in molasses," she says.

"You right."

"You so busy sucking it up, you don't know you're going down until your ass begins to disappear."

"Yes, ma'am."

Back Home Again in Indiana

We stumble at the door of the Tin Roof Café, Doc holding me up, falling into bright lights and hot Dixieland jazz. We find a table close to the high, wooden stage, drinking Turbo Dogs, taking it all in.

The place jumps. And there's no turning back because I've got a job to do here tonight.

Lao Tsu says, "Go with the present."

The Old Buzzards Jass Band is the brainchild of local genius Johnny "Buzzerhead" Smith who plays piano and surrounds himself with some old cats who really know how to play, like Suds Lafitte on standup bass. There's a young woman, twenty, twenty-one, a jazz student visiting from Sweden, and they invite her clarinet up on stage. It's all very shy peaches and cream, she's very polite, eyes looking around, young blonde Nordic innocent charm deferring to the gentlemen, and the guys kind of chuckle along and do their brilliant bits, benignly, but after a couple of numbers, Johnny nods, and I step up to the stage with my sweet horn and blow two sweet notes, and the young woman relaxes into a girl again, stepping back into that vibratile, sacred place where her very first notes were played as a child, and the whole band begins to jell as we kick into "Back Home Again in Indiana."

I grew up in Indiana, a dirty crossroads town. I was thinking about my mom and all her dirty tricks, and boy, was my horn sweet. I don't know what the young woman on the clarinet was thinking, but she was blowing crystallized, straight ahead purity.

Just keep talking to me, baby.

Buzzerhead, Suds, the blonde, and all the rest of us rocked the whole set, the bar moving Turbo Dogs like buckets in a fire brigade, the band on fire, Johnny setting eighty-eight fires with his classy, incendiary honkytonk stride, and the whole band followed, fire chasers, running every red light, lighting fireworks, spiders on fire, all night long, blowing hot and blowing sweet.

And I was back home again in Indiana.

Three in the morning, and falling down from the bandstand after handshakes all around and a big hug from Johnny, my hand was taken by the young woman, and she led me through the bar to the men's restroom. She pushed me hard in the lower back into the pissy, vomity room, and closing the door behind us, she threw a deadbolt to lock us in. She unzipped my pants, reached in, grabbed hold of my cock and pulled it out of my pants. She put her lips around the tip and began to pump, playing me like a slide, all seven positions, on a well-oiled slide trombone. She played me like a trumpet, the Miles Davis of cocksuckers, and I swelled into an ivory clarinet, a big mouth full, a young Swedish blonde giving a broken-down, crazy trumpet player head, and I came shaking and shuddering, pumping jump jass to the jazz of her reedless, sucking mouth.

She swallowed all.

A real good player.

"You're a sweet horn," she said.

III

The Yellow Backhoe

Amazing how we persist with all the sour rituals beside the certain, measurable knowledge that no one moment has the least continuity with the next. Lewis opens his eyes to the glaring day, and he finds himself sitting on the back porch, leaning with his back against the door of the house.

Naked again. Why does life keep repeating itself?

Getting up on his feet, he almost falls on his face but manages to brace himself against the door, which is locked.

Knocks.

"Doc."

Knocks.

Doc must not be at home, or he's passed out in his bedroom and can't hear. Knocks again, hitting the door, *smack smack smack*, with both palms open.

A Public Works Dept yellow backhoe is digging a deep trench the width of the street at the foot of the driveway. A radio playing in the tractor cab blares like a loudspeaker:

> " . . . *You don't know what love is*
> *Until you face the night with sleepless eyes* . . ."

Rayanne dePaul wrote that song, and he wonders why, walking around the side of the house at this troubled moment in his life, he remembers that fact. Jumps up and bangs on the shuttered windows above his head.

No answer.

Back to the front porch.

There's a case of empty bottles. He goes through them, bottle by bottle. Two or three have an ounce of leftover beer. Checks for floating butts and drinks the warm sour swill.

"Mercy."

Hiccough, hiccough.

Nausea.

A bottle slips out of his hands and breaks on the pavement. Gets down on his hands and knees above the random scatter of brown glass fragments and dry heaves. Slivers of sunlight scatter through the folds of his brain like traces of hog toenail in a sausage.

In the street, the yellow backhoe roars, chokes, almost stalls, backfires, and continues to dig. The work is random, without reason, and thorough. The extending bucket veers haphazardly left and right and drops its steel teeth deeply into the oyster-shell loam. A mounting levee of sand and shell builds up against the rear bumper of Doc's car. A water pipe suddenly bursts, and the trench rapidly fills with dank, sour sewer water.

That's when he sees Ms Sugar sitting in the bucket seat of the cab, at the controls of the yellow backhoe.

"Hey," he says.

Running naked down the driveway.

"Come here," he says.

Ms Sugarlicq wrestles with the steering wheel. The tractor spins an awkward donut in the street. She pulls down hard at a lever. The bucket swings around wildly in the air, jerking up and down.

"Baby doll," he says, standing at the edge of the trench that bubbles with souring, brown water.

The tractor roars, its wheels turn, the bucket extends forward like a battering ram and charges straight ahead at Lewis. He runs back to the house and pounds on the door. The bucket hits the edge of the porch, snapping a ten-inch column like a toothpick. Slate shingles fall from the roof of the porch at his feet, and he presses up close against the wall of the house.

The yellow backhoe shifts into reverse, retreats to the street, turns and chugs away, the bucket swinging like a pendulum left and right. Taking a sharp left turn at the end of the block, Ms Sugar leans out of the cab and waves goodbye.

And now the door opens.

Doc is buttoning up a brand-new shirt, and I have an impulse to *bury my nose in that snowy expanse of soft finespun cotton.*

"What the hell is going on?" says Doc.

"I need some clothes."

I push Doc out of the way and step into the house. The radio in the living room is on:

" . . . *You don't know what love is* . . ."

Bunkhouse Blowjob

Don't ever try to control a woman. Trying to control a woman is like trying to control the energy of the universe. It can't be done. She will come around or not come around, but there is nothing you can do. You are unimportant because there is always another cock.

Lewis walks around the block. He discovers the yellow backhoe, abandoned and turned on its side, a grotesque carcass of giant machinery at the bottom of a huge hole of sour water. Further up, there's a small Public Works Dept bunkhouse built of board and batten like a small shotgun house sitting on four large, balloon tires parked in the middle of the street. There's not enough room for cars to get around it without driving up on one side or the other of the broken banquette.

The door of the bunkhouse is open and someone, a workman, is sitting just inside. He's eating a banana.

"Suck it, bitch, suck it."

This at screaming volume over two loudspeakers perched atop the eaves of the bunkhouse.

Lewis walks closer.

The bunkhouse door slams shut.

"Oh, oh, oh."

A woman's voice over the loud speaker, Ms S.

"Suck it."

"Oh."

"Suck it."

"Oh."

"Suck."

"Oh, yes."

"Oh, baby."

"Yes, yes, yes."

Standing in the middle of the street, on fire like a struck match, I freeze, aflame, and the sweat pours. I sprout horns. Spit bile. My brains sizzle and fry to a crumbly carbon.

A shovel is in my hands.

I swing it in the air and knock out a loudspeaker.

"Yes, yes . . ."

I swing again at the second speaker, hitting it square, and the street is quiet.

I knock at the door.

The door of the shotgun bunkhouse opens, and a workman, the eater of the banana, pokes his head out. Pulled over his dirty blue coveralls, he's wearing a Lewis King T-shirt.

I let him have it, the back of the shovel blade to the side of his head which immediately caves in like a rotten pumpkin. Pieces of teeth and gums and blood splatter my shirt and face. I'm spitting jagged bits of enamel and his hot blood.

The workman drops dead at my feet.

Hands on knees. Breathing hard.

Listening to the mockingbirds in the trees sing.

No traffic.

Nobody on the banquette.

Nobody runs out of their shotgun house howling cold-blooded murder.

Two blocks away, a St Charles Avenue streetcar passes by.

Maybe nobody saw me do this.

I try to pull off the T-shirt, but he's too fat, I can't even move his fat arms. I shovel sand against the dead workman's face, covering his shattered head. I dance around the dead body, kicking and shovelling sand. It takes exactly two minutes and ten seconds to completely cover the body. Except for his big butt.

I give up.

I look up and down the street.

Is there anybody alive in New Orleans?

I hear a squeak and turn to the bunkhouse. Crawling through the door, the place is empty. Nobody's here. I look around: tools, black plastic pipe, porno mags, banana peels. No place in here really to hide anywhere, I can barely turn around, only one door and no windows. So where's Ms Sugar?

Squeak. Squeak.

On a small table that folds down from the wall is a cassette tape player. A tape is playing out to its end.

I hit the stop button.

I rewind it.

Squeak. Squeak.

Hit "play."

"Suck it, bitch, suck it."

"Oh, oh, oh."

"Suck it."

"Oh."

"Suck it."
"Oh."
"Suck."
"Oh, yes."
"Oh, baby."
"Yes, yes, yes."

Hair of the Dog

Doc pours two big tumblers of Wild Turkey, and we drink them down straight.

"Okay," he says.

"You right."

Doc pours, and we drink another round.

The kitchen spins like a top.

"How deep did you bury the body?" he says.

"He's on the fucking street."

"Take the crawfish six weeks to eat him there," he says.

"Right."

"We better rebury him," he says.

Doc helps me drag the dead workman's body into the front yard.

"Start digging," he says.

We're standing inside the police tape where the first workman's body was found.

"Here?"

"Cops will never cross the line," says Doc. "Trust me."

I dig with the shovel that killed the workman.

Three feet deep, the sudsy, brown water begins bubbling to the surface.

"I'll get a colander," says Doc.

He runs off to the house.

Four feet deep, I have to stop. There's more water than sandy mud on the shovel. I'm not going to go any deeper.

Doc gets down on his knees to dip in his colander, catching crawfish with each swipe.

"Supper," he says.

We roll the workman's dead body into the man-sized hole filling with sour, brown water, and the splash dirties my shoes and the cuffs of my pants.

The corpse bobs in the filthy water. The crawfish are already moving in.

"A floater," says Doc.

"Where's his fucking T-shirt?"

"What T-shirt?"

"He was wearing my T-shirt."

"I don't know," says Doc. "Fill him in."

I take up the shovel and with the first scoop, *splat,* cover the dead workman's stiff and sullen face. The second scoop glances off his fat torso and splashes into the water. The third scoop is a thump of wet sand on dead flesh, and the body, finally, begins to slowly sink in its watery grave.

I take a deep breath.

A long sigh.

And then, I fill him in.

Dirty Sex

Lewis dirty, stinking and sweaty from his grave digging, his clothes soaked in shit and blood and sour earth, pokes his head into the bedroom. Ms S is on the bed naked, masturbating, smelling of lilacs and come.

"When did you get in?" I say.
"Last night, stupid."
"You've been here all night?"
"Missing you."
"What about the backhoe?"
"Backhoe?"
She doesn't know what I'm talking about.
"Where have you been?" she says.
"I had to do some things."
"Come here."
"I'm all dirty."
"I like dirty sometimes."
"I was going to take a shower."

"I want to suck your dirty cock."

Which begins to harden in my filthy pants.

I take a step towards the end of the bed. She reaches up and cups my ass cheeks in her hands, unzips my pants with her teeth, taking my hard and dirty cock into her mouth, the tongue licking me up and down, kissing the mushroom rim with chicken pecks, driving me crazy, deep throat, soft throat, throat of silk and come . . . abruptly taking her mouth and tongue and sharp knives of kisses away to catch her breath.

"Oh, god," I say.

My pants fall to the floor.

"Don't get used to this," she says.

"What?"

"Me being so nice to you."

"This all about?"

"You're not important," she says.

My hard cock curls into a limp worm.

"Happy to see me?" she says.

I turn away.

She grabs my arm.

"Going take a shower," I say.

"Fuck you," she says. "Fuck you."

"Okay," I say. "Just let me go."

"Little boy loses to a girl?" she says.

"Yeah right," I say.

She sticks the middle finger of her right hand up my asshole.

"Who do you think you are?" she says.

I let the tissues of my asshole relax around the muscles of her finger. Feels good.

"Who do you think you are?"

"Nobody," I say.

"Wrong answer," she says, removing the finger.

The Garden District

I slip in the shower, land on my ass and hit my head hard against the edge of the tub. I cut myself twice shaving. And go downstairs to join everybody in the kitchen, loudly talking up the brand new day with Doc and Judy and Ms Sugarlicq: chicory coffee, burned grits, fried bread and *The Times Picayune* for our breakfast. Ms Sugar sits on my lap the whole time, squirming around, biting my neck, making me hard and wet, and she curls up with her head on my chest and her arms around my neck.

"I love you, honey," she says.

"I love you, too."

"You guys got a bedroom upstairs," says Doc.

"I love this man," says Ms Sugar.

She kisses my lips with a bite of teeth.

"We're apposite, not opposite," she says.

"Yeah right," says Doc.

"That means we're side by side."

"I know what it means," he says.

Doc reaches into the cupboard and pulls out a bottle of Wild Turkey. He waggles it at me.

"Ready?"

"Yeah right," I say.

"Why do you have to drink all the time?" says Ms S.

"I got a lot on my mind, honey," I say.

"I want to play today," she says.

Ms Sugar snuggles my neck.

"Yeah right."

I drink the tumbler of whiskey down. And signal Doc to pour me another.

Ms S and I ride the bicycles through Audubon Park and down Camp Street, heading downtown, crossing Napoleon Avenue, Louisiana Avenue, Washington Avenue, but stopping frequently along the way to look at all the grand houses and a Gothic-style church, St Stephen Cathedral built in 1849, at Camp & Napoleon. We comb the Garden District street by street but can't locate the home of Anne Rice, Ms Sugar's favourite writer. Doc's directions scribbled on an envelope are pretty vague. We begin asking passersby on the street for directions, but they're all obvious tourists too and don't know a thing, walking around lost, confused, flipping through their guidebooks, no one knowing for sure where they are, even what street they're on, suddenly pointing ahead and running off like a gaggle of geese.

"This way," they all say.

We see a young couple dressed in black and silver clothes, snooping around a large house at the southeast corner of First Street and Chestnut. They're sharing a Camel filter cigarette.

"This is it," they say.

239 First Street.

Ms Sugar takes several pictures of the house, a dark green New Orleans classic with white columns two storeys high; dark, shuttered windows, white wicker furniture on the second floor portico; plus pictures of the painted-black, wrought iron fence. The slate slab banquette in front, the brass plate on the front gate that says "Deliveries To Side Gate"; the deep, rich flame of green lawn in the withering sunlight; the white marble nude who pours fresh water from a marble jug into the marble fountain encircled by geometrically-arranged plantings of bloodred flowers.

I take one of Sugar in front of the closed gate. She looks good in black. From here on the street it's hard to tell, but hovering in front of the door to the house, directly behind Ms Sugar's right shoulder—is that a small angel fashioned from the purity of grief or just an illusion of the day's reflected sunlight?

I lean down through the wrought iron fence to pick a wild purplish flower, a slip of pale lavender tissue that immediately turns shit brown in my hands. I try to save it, a souvenir for Ms Sugar, by pressing it between two pages of sheet music in the trumpet case. Snapping the case shut, a sudden sharp, hot pain runs up my arm. My chest heaves. There's an ocean of nausea throughout my body. My hands begin to tremble and wrinkle, turning crisply brown like drying tobacco leaves. Drops of blood squeeze out from beneath my fingernails, pooling at the tips of all ten fingers. What is it? Leprosy? The Black Plague?

"Are you coming?" says Ms Sugar.

I'm down on all fours.

"Can't breathe," I say.

"You shouldn't have picked that flower."

I struggle to open the trumpet case and barely have enough strength left to throw the faded flower back over the fence. It falls to the ground with a thud like a stone.

Ms S takes off in a sprint down Chestnut Street, and I get on my bike and try my best to keep up, wobbling far behind. We ride the bikes almost downtown, passing all the streets named for the muses: Polymnia, Euterpe, Terpsichore,

Melpomene, Thalia, Erato, turning around abruptly at Clio when Ms Sugar finds a piece of hammered gold in the middle of the street and picks it up, an antique earring in the shape of a coiled snake.

"Good luck," she says.

"Yeah right."

"You're the one who picked the flower."

We ride back again through the Garden District, Ms S insisting on traversing a cross both ways several blocks deep and wide, Magazine Street to St Charles Avenue, and Jackson Avenue to Louisiana, with our axis at Lafayette Cemetery, which is walled all around in crumbly, white-washed brick, and whose rusting iron gates are locked to the public with chain and heavy padlocks. Ms S climbs on top of the wall of the cemetery to take some pictures.

"There's a man running around in there," she says.

I look through the iron bars of the locked gate.

A figure is running, trying not to be seen, between graves toward the far side of the cemetery.

"Looks like Paul," I say.

And it is Paul. He stops between two graves and looks right at me.

"Catch me if you can," he says.

He leans down to touch his toes with his hands and turns a complete backflip. He pirouettes gracefully across a stone slab, and, agile as a monkey, scampers out of sight behind a tomb. I climb the high, white wall and jump down into the cemetery, my shoes sinking an inch into the shelly sod.

"Paul."

I walk behind the tomb. He's gone.

"Paul."

I look around, walk behind another tomb.

Nobody here.

Except me. And the anciently dead.

I climb back over the wall.

Ms Sugarlicq and her bicycle are gone.

I ride around looking for her, finally riding out of the Garden District, crossing Magazine Street, and a block riverside, discover her bicycle locked to a street sign in the blistering sunlight outside Parasol's Bar, which is no more than a shack with a rusting tin roof, the toilets overflowing with turds and sopping wads of dirty toilet paper on the floor, but sitting down on a stool at the tiny, dark, air-conditioned bar I find a cold and welcoming longneck of beer and an unwelcoming Ms Sugar, talking New Orleans to a drunken cook who's jawing about going broke ten years ago on a tuna boat off the coast of California and washing dishes in the rain forest, Portland, Seattle, Vancouver, inviting her to come down and try his restaurant, one of Emeril's, very high class, saying she won't walk away disappointed, and vaguely promises Ms Sugarlicq a trip to Baton Rouge for some really good roux, but only if she's willing to leave immediately, this afternoon, as soon as he returns from taking a leak.

"You're thinking of going?" I say.

"Why not," she says. "There's nothing I want here."

Outside the bar, unlocking the bicycles, Ms Sugar says she has to take a pee and goes back inside. Nearby, a young girl is sitting on the front porch stoop of a deep purple shotgun house. Friendly and outfront, cute as magnolia, sweet as bread pudding, and maybe fourteen years old, she hustles me to contribute to her school yearbook, a fundraiser. I give her a dollar and ask her name.

"Delphinia," she says.

"That's a pretty name."

"Two dollars get you a kiss."

"How much for a hug?"

"Fifty cents, I reckon."

"Yeah right."

"Well?"

She gets up from the steps and stretches her arms over her head.

"Afternoon, Delphinia."

"Watcha waitin for?" she says.

She puts her hands on her hips and stretches forward.

"Say hi to your momma and dem," I say.

She laughs.

"You waitin' for yur girlfriend?"

"Yeah."

"She's fuckin' the cook in the toilet."

"What?"

"You heared me the furst time."

"What you know about it?"

"Voodoo," she says. "I'm clairvoyant."

❦

Ms S walks out of Parasol's Bar, on the cook's arm. Lewis falls down on his face, bloodying his nose, his upper lip and his chin. He is ugly and disgusting.

"You are ugly and disgusting," says Ms S.

. . . returning home all the way down darkening Magazine Street . . . lined with bars and restaurants and antique shops . . . the architecture a gumbo of styles and eras but all of it crumbling, charming in decay . . . the street full of potholes and sunset traffic blaring by . . . the day frying its egg over the river, the air beginning to cool.

A little boy waves on the darkening banquette.

"Hello, bike riders," he says.

We cycle into the black oaks of Audubon Park, dissolving into darkness.

Back at Doc's place, putting away the bicycles, Doc and Judy are going out the door, off to get a bite to eat at some Mexican dive uptown on Maple Street.

"What the hell happened to you?" Doc says to me.

"Teenage hooker," says Ms Sugar.

"They're a hazard," says Doc.

Ms Sugar and I are pretty worn out by our long day and decide to take a nap, making love for an hour in the dark, like cats, biting, scratching, screaming, no holds barred. We get into the shower together. I soap her up and scrub her down, all but her ankles and feet, and we laugh about that. She soaps up a washcloth and tenderly washes my bloody face, my bloody nose, upper lip and chin.

"Oh, honey," she says.

"Right."

"It's just like Faye Dunaway and Jack Nicholson."

Rock 'n' Bowl

Doc and Judy return, and the four of us go out to Rock 'n' Bowl, an old bowling alley dancehall, the one and only original museum of kitsch and two-step, built in the '40s, offering authentic deep-fried "Louisiana cuisine" in the kitchen. We're going to catch some zydeco.

The band is a washtub, a squeezebox, a drumkit, four—count them—guitars, and a female singer. Too much catgut for my taste. Where am I supposed to squeeze in with my horn? Pretty good singer though . . . "*les flammes d'enver*" . . . we all dance and jump and laugh, except Ms Sugarlicq who is tired and confused and confusing. People whirling around us, she slumps on my shoulder, says she wants to go away.

"Fuck, I'm supposed to play here," I say.

"Who cares?" says Ms Sugar.

"This is how I make my living."

"What living?" says Ms Sugar.

So we compromise and go to the food booth where we order a crawfish quesadilla and a side of deep-fried alligator. I guzzle a couple Abita Reds from plastic cups, and then we stand around and watch people dance and bowl. In fact, everybody in the building is either dancing or bowling, except for us locked in the vague exclusivity of Ms

Sugar's worldview. And then Ms Sugar wants to dance again, but it's not what I would call dancing but public frottage mixed with intimate deep throat kisses in the middle of the roaring room of two-step zydeco and sweat. When the band tries to pull me up on stage, I shake my head.

"No, not tonight."

And I walk away out the door into the parking lot.

On the way downtown to some blues bar after midnight, Ms Sugarlicq wants to get out of the car, and Doc lurches to a stop at the side of the street, waiting for her to get out.

"Well?" says Doc.

"I'm with her," I say.

"Two gigs you fucked me up on tonight," says Doc.

He's more than a little pissed off.

Ms Sugar and I get out of the car and stand around beneath the levee near the bend in the Mississippi River at Hampson Street. Doc drives away to more drinking and dancing, and more than likely adding up the cost of my stay in New Orleans.

Ms Sugar thinks she's hungry again, but the Camellia Grill is too bright and the Trolley Stop Café is too dark. She only wants to eat in all the places that are closed.

"What does you wants, baby?" I say.

Nothing but contradiction.

Finally walking ahead of me down Hampson Street to Doc's place, she says she's sad, thinking about all the people who have disappeared from her life.

"Talk to me," I say.

But she can't vocalize more than a few, disconnected words in random, unfinished sentences, some of which lack nouns and others have no verb. All are nonsense. I'm utterly confused, don't quite understand anything she's saying, and I get sensitive, defensive.

"A lot of men have died in my life," she says.

"They were the lucky ones."

"Fuck you, shithead," she says.

She runs off down the broken banquette.

I let her go. I've got the key to the house and find her five minutes later sitting on the step of Doc's porch.

I have to laugh.

"What's really going on here?" I say.

Barely get the words out of my mouth, and I slip in dogshit, trip over the police tape barrier and sink two feet into the fresh grave of the workman that I had murdered with the shovel blade that morning.

"Shit," I say.

There's mud and water up to my knees. It sucks at me like quicksand. My shoes collapse into something solid to push off against, and a bubble the size of a pancake explodes through the mud, splattering bits of shit on my face. Ms Sugar laughs as I scramble out of the grave onto more solid ground.

"What's so god damned funny?"

"You are," she says.

"Fuck."

"All you do is swear," she says. "And drink."

"This isn't about you."

I sit down on the porch stoop beside her and try to clean my shoes with tufts of grass pulled up from the yard.

"Let me in," she says.

I unlock the door for her. I take off my filthy shoes and prop them dripping wet against the house. Inside, Ms Sugar is pouting on the couch. I walk past her into the kitchen, my wet socks making sucking noises on the worn carpet, and get a beer from the fridge. I try to talk to her, but she's angry, yelling and accusing me of never letting her have her way, have her say. She screams her way upstairs to the bedroom. I go back to the kitchen and drink another beer.

A tumbler of whiskey.

And yet another beer.

I go upstairs, take my clothes off and get into bed with her. But she won't talk except to yell and curse me.

"Let's try to get some sleep," I say.

She sits up in bed.

"Fuck me," she says.

I take her in my arms, and we make love, sweetly, tenderly, in complete silence, except to pledge everlasting love to one another as our orgasms rush forward like two strands of one river joining together. We are a man and a woman going to hell in New Orleans. I am her man, and she is my woman.

"I love you."

"I love you, too."

She goes to sleep about three in the morning, the grating buzz of the air conditioner doing all the talking now, the blankets thrown off the end of the bed onto the floor. Two naked people share a bed without touching.

The radio is on.

"It's 3:31, but so what?" says the deejay. "Some place it's 4:31."

Mother's Day

Lazing about with Ms Sugar, making love and sweet whispers into the heat of the day, 94° in the shade, lying side by side on the bed in the chattering air-conditioned room.

We go for a walk down Maple Street, take a slow, hungover browse through the white clapboard shotgun house that is Maple Leaf Books, black and white photos of Mark Twain, William Faulkner, Walker Percy, and John Kennedy Toole on the wall spaces between books. Go to a drugstore to buy bottled water and a container of codeine-laced tylenol and walk back, making love again, side by side, enjoying the hot day and the flames of sex, burning up consciousness.

"I love you."

"I love you, too."

We catch the streetcar and ride it to Canal Street, walking the full length of Bourbon Street with a sidebar stop at 726 St Peter Street, in front of Preservation Hall.

"This is where it all began," I say.

"Where what began?" says Ms S.

"The birthplace of jazz," I say. "Kid Ory, King Oliver, Sidney Bechet, they all came through those doors."

"Looks like a bomb hit it," she says.

I take out my trumpet and play an impromptu solo, but my lips are dry, my nerves fried, and a biker in front of a bar across the street asks me unkindly to shut the fuck up.

Dozens of bikers, in leather, tattoos, scowls, cigarettes and beer, plus lots of cops, observe the passing scene. Music assaults from left and right out of the afternoon bars, hard rock, deep blues, trad jazz, backbeat funk.

Bikers surround Lewis. He charms them with his sweet horn.

Everybody dancing in the street.

The cops tapping their feet.

The guy who told Lewis to shut the fuck up buys him a three-for-one drink.

Crossing St Philips Street past Lafitte's Blacksmith Shop, Bourbon Street becomes residential, and suddenly it's like we're the only two people in the whole French Quarter, *a little piece of eternity dropped into your hands—and who knows what to do with it?*

Walking riverside Esplanade Avenue, magnificent third-floor iron-wrought balcony apartment buildings glow in the evening sun, floating above the shadowy, big sprawling oaks with multiple trunks like hardwood octopi, giant limbs akimbo. Green floppy bushes flower pink flames spreading over neutral ground. A Parish of Orleans firetruck idles, hoses running off in all directions, seemingly abandoned in the middle of the street.

"Maybe we're the only two people left in the world," says Ms Sugarlicq.

We cut across Chartres to Frenchmen Street, and out of nowhere a swooping bird flies directly across my face, grazing my cheek, and a delicious, ghostly snatch of "Funky Butt Blues" sears the early evening air like a slicing hiss of burning fat. It was on this street, while leading the Labor Day Parade in September, 1907, that Buddy Bolden, the hot pepper genius daddy of the jass cornet, blew his brains out through the bell of his horn. He spent the rest of his days in an insane asylum. I touch my cheek, wiping away a bubble of blood, get down on all fours and kiss the sacred pavement of the street.

"God bless."

I taste my blood, salt hot.

"What are you doing?" says Ms S.

Getting up on my feet again, I pat out a chorus of funky butt, a finger-tapping blues, on my trumpet case.

May the music never die.

Walking past Checkpoint Charlie's, a combination laundromat and licensed jazz club, we find The Praline Connection restaurant on the next corner. Doc and Judy already have a table inside, a perfect table because it's both close to a screen door of cooling evening air, and also close to the kitchen. The four of us feast on a supper of hot biscuits and syrup, fried chicken and gravy, red beans and rice, okra, potato salad, BBQ ribs, hot peppers and big, frosty jugs of Abita Red.

It's Mother's Day, and all of us talk about how our mother made fried chicken or potato salad or pecan pie. Everybody, that is, except me.

"Well, Lewis?" says Doc.

"My mother never cooked anything," I say.

"Yeah right."

"Well, she fried up a rat once."

Everybody stops eating and puts their fork down on their plate. They all look at me.

"I don't want to talk about it."

I order another jug of Abita Red.

Half a block up the street from Washington Square on Frenchmen Street is a club called Snug Harbor where Ellis Marsalis plays every Friday night. We go into the dark bar and along the long corridor to the back room where floor to ceiling mirrors cling to the high walls. We find a high, round table in the corner by the door and order beers. It's snug in here all right. Forty people make the room a tight squeeze.

There's a six-piece band fronted by a young torch singer with a big voice and a bigger butt, who lives in Paris, France, who belts it out, sentimental, autobiographical ballads about lost love and tender moms and dead friends, and it's a good thing that a damn good band is backing her up, piano, bass, sax, drum, percussion, and me on my sweet horn.

I can't stand up for long, and somebody gets me a chair, but my horn is sweet, the torch singer is sweet, and the band follows her behind for three sets of fat, sweet jazz. On a break, I stagger through the crowded room. There's a sign in the men's restroom: "The 11th Commandment— Thou Shalt Not Commit Adulthood."

On the street between sets, Ms Sugar and I hang out, talking and laughing with the band and their fans, two or three in the crowd are legitimate mothers even and everybody gives them a round of applause. There's a thin, wirey guy from Colorado who says his grandfather lives in

Victoria. Do we know Parry Street? Another guy talks about the cost of living in New Orleans.

"Rent's okay," he says, "as long as you're dead and floating in your grave."

Everybody laughs and coughs on their cigarettes.

"New Orleans is five feet under water," he says. "If you dig a hole, it's going to fill up."

Another guy is the father of the singer, and his butt is even bigger than hers. Does this mean anything? The big butt singer with the sweet voice wants me to come with her to Paris and arrange her charts.

"Come, come, oh, yes, do come," she says.

She leans her head on my shoulder and turns her pleasant face up to mine. She squeals.

"Well . . . are you coming?" she says.

We're lips to lips, less than a quiver of flesh from touching.

"I'd have to bring my girlfriend."

"Forget the girlfriend."

She runs her right hand up the crotch of my pants.

"I'm in love with that woman over there," I say.

Ms Sugarlicq is french kissing with the guy from Colorado.

"Love is blind," says the singer.

"No, I see it all," I say.

Later we walk through the whole fucking French Quarter, looking for Doc's car. He forgot where he parked, and it takes us two hours to find it. Ms Sugar wants to take a cab but doesn't have any money, and I won't give her any. She can come home with the rest of us. She's got it so tough, she can get down here on the pavement with me. I'm crawling on all fours.

We get back to Doc's about four in the morning.

Everybody goes to bed, one by one clomping up the stairs to the bedrooms, only I can't go to sleep, keep turning over despite counting like sheep the rhythmic slap of spanks resounding through the house from Doc's bedroom.

Sleeping and waking and dreaming . . . far away a hauntingly forlorn train whistle drifts through the night, blowing one lonesome note of pure jazz, one long unrequited moan for this or that pleasure of the flesh . . . forlorn steel cry of wheel against steel against hardwood tie against gravel against the hard earth, and in the dark of the quiet room . . . tracing my lover's body with my right index fingernail . . . toe to ankle to calf to knee to thigh to hip to breast to shoulder and over the back all the way ever so slowly, gently over each curving indentation of the spine . . . perfume and flesh and dream in the darkest hour of the night . . . I slip my tongue tip, tender lick and suck, curling tiny blonde hairs all over her body . . . electrical celebration of two lovers next to one window that so slowly begins to brighten to the colour of a camellia flower . . . and somewhere nearby a wild bird sings—what is the name of that bird that sings—joining together the lonely ache in everyone, sweetly shuddering dawn in New Orleans.

"I'll try to stay away from other guys for a while," says Ms Sugarlicq.

Impressions of New Orleans

(for solo trumpet)

Big muddy shotgun shack
    razor wire
    rooster crow
river bend
    jazz radio
       floating cloud

the spirit of
    Louis Armstrong
all that's left of Storyville
    on a broken brick wall
a little bird
    inside-out with song

crawfish & corn bisque
    sweet
       sunlight
in a piping bowl

oak tree hung
        with Spanish moss
& a rope swing
        swinging boy
shouts *hello*

Trolley Stop Café
        "stop for some beers"
salt pea!
nuts!
        salt pea!
        nuts!
shells
        & then my chin
        across the portico

camellia midnight's
        sweet
scent fills
in the
fuckin
        potholes

Pallet on the Floor

We lock the bicycles against a burning, sunlit wall on the broken banquette in front of a coffee shop, PJ's uptown on Maple Street. Mid-morning birds sing in the hanging gardens on the outside deck where at tables the smart college girls stretch like beautiful cats in the sun, talking comedy and tragedy, truth and beauty and poetry.

Ms Sugar happily scrawls a dozen "wish you were here" postcards to her many lovers back home, all the time touching my arm, whispering close.

"I love you," she says.

"I love you, too."

"No, you, I love you," she says.

And goes back to perfuming her postcards.

I chew on capsules of generic tylenol with codeine, tossing half a dozen into my mouth like peanuts, chalk white, crunchy as hard candy, bitter as cooling rage. I take out my notebook from the trumpet case, open it and ponder cold-blooded murder, working on a melody for a song about killing a man with a shovel.

Ms S reads over my shoulder.

"You have an active imagination," she says.

"Yeah right."

Out in the street, a New Orleans Police Dept squad car is driving slowly past, the lollipop cop at the wheel, and he's looking right at us.

"Jesus christ," I say.

"What?" says Ms S.

"Your cop boyfriend."

"I think he's cute," she says.

"Don't fucking wave."

She waves.

The squad car passes out of sight.

We ride the bicycles back to Doc's house. The squad car is parked out in front, the engine running. The lollipop cop is standing on the front porch, knocking on the door.

He doesn't see us.

"Keep riding," I say.

Ms Sugarlicq stops in the middle of the street, and I rearend her, sending us both flying off our bikes.

The lollipop cop stands over me, the fingers of his right hand tapping a two-step backbeat against the bone handle of his still-holstered revolver.

"Hi," says Ms Sugarlicq.

"Hi," he says.

"Well, help me up," she says.

The lollipop cop helps her up.

I get up on my own and pick up the trumpet case.

"Freeze."

His revolver is drawn.

"How's your momma and dem?" I say.

"What's going on here?" he says.

"We're from Canada," I say.

"Canada?"

"Up north."

He scratches his head with the barrel of his gun.

"Foreigners?"

"American."

"But you're living in that there Canada?"

"Yeah right."

"That's kind of un-American."

"May I?"

I snap the latches on the trumpet case and open it.

"Easy."

I show him my passport.

He looks at it upside down. The man can't read.

He hands it back.

"Where's yours, ma'am?" he says.

"In the toolshed," says Ms Sugar.

"Toolshed?"

"There's a pallet on the floor," she says.

The lollipop cop is confused.

"Mississippi John Hurt," I say.

"Huh?"

"Guy that wrote the song."

"Yeah right."

On the way to the toolshed, we pass by the shallow grave. The yellow police tape is collapsing under the weight of a fresh pile of muddy earth and broken shell. Someone has dug up the dead workman and removed the body. It's now just another hole in the ground where crawfish frolic in the filthy water.

Ms S steps into the toolshed and turns around.

"Well, come on in and close the door," she says.

"Don't go anywhere," he says to me.

The lollipop cop steps into the toolshed and closes the door behind him, leaving me alone.

Click.

The kitchen side porch door opens, and Doc throws our bags out on the pavement of the driveway.

"What's up, Doc?"

"You're fired," he says.

Doc slams the door in my face and locks it shut from inside with the deadbolt. I hammer the door with my fists.

"Doc."

Gunshot.

I fall to the ground. The toolshed door swings open, and the lollipop cop steps out. The police revolver in his hand is smoking. The fly on his pants is undone. He walks past where I lie whimpering, prostrate, my nose pressed flat into a grouted groove between two bricks in the driveway.

"Try to stay out of trouble," he says.

He struts to the idling squad car, throws the revolver down on the front seat, zips up his pants, and gets in behind the wheel. He drives away down the street, making a sharp right at the next block before turning on the siren.

I get up slowly and walk to the toolshed.

Ms Sugar is on her knees, buttoning up her blouse.

"Whatever," she says.

Lafitte's Blacksmith Shop

Stopped here for a beer, the corner of St Philips and Bourbon, following a stumbling pilgrimage with Ms S lakeside up Canal, the widest street in America. Dingy shops, dirty banquette, razor blue cops on horseback, overflowing trashcans, and yesterday's newspaper faces, the citizens of New Orleans eating ice creams and po'boys and humble pie, spitting up hopelessness and bile, jazz and sex and snake eyes, everybody going to heaven, everybody going to hell, and we cross and turn downtown onto legendary Basin Street, but the marching bands have all vanished in the smog, the fat tubas nothing but roadkill under the wheels of thunder rolling off Interstate 10.

I slip and fall on the greasy banquette, getting up slowly in front of sly stares, three boys bouncing a basketball against a dismal redbrick slum wall in The Projects. Taking Ms Sugar's hand, one slow step at a time, first the right shoe, then the left shoe, and we shuffle through the iron gates into walled St Louis Cemetery No.1.

Ms Sugarlicq takes snapshots of all the monuments and the tombs, the charcoal crosses scrawled over marble, amulets, relics, keepsakes, tarnished crucifixes, tiny plaster idols, stones placed down in a pattern: triangles; crosses;

plastic flowers; a string of fake pearls in a marble vase, crumbly mortar, old brick; a scab of green grass between two tombs, white walls, iron gates, catacombs, the white haze of sky shrouding the downtown skyscrapers of New Orleans.

A woman lies on a marble bed with her small marble child across her body, both recently departed, and at the foot of the marble bed, the broken marble husband kneels.

"For the virtuous there is a better world."

Ms S climbs up on top of a thin slab of white marble long and wide enough to hold her body, supported like a table over six elegant white marble columns. She lies down along the length of the white slab like a body in state with her arms folded across her chest with clasped hands. In the hot sunlight, she looks carved out of marble.

"The graves shall give up their dead."

Facing east for the resurrection of Christ—head propped up on trumpet case—I slump on the ground in the hot sun between two sets of catacombs honey-combed three graves high, the mouths of some chambers sealed up with marble slabs bearing inscriptions . . . *"Qui, qui tu sois, respecte ce monument, dernier asile d'une fille bonne et vertueuse"* . . . others cheap brick and broken plaster without any indication of the person's name occupying it, and two of the lower tombs are open. A freshly-dug grave right beside me is slowly filling with water. *All in New Orleans are buried in water.*

A brass band consisting of trumpet, tuba, tenor saxophone, bass drum, cymbal, snare drum and trombone, playing

"Swing Low, Sweet Chariot," and six pallbearers dressed in white suits, white shirts, ties, hats, carrying a shiny, black casket overhead, and leading a ragged procession: a pastor in a black suit and white collar, armed with a Bible, followed by a dozen moaning mourners, mostly middle-aged women shrouded head to toe in black, each carrying a lit candle in the sun, pass through the heavy iron gates into the white-walled sanctuary wherein the dead may be said to rest in peace.

The procession crosses between the tombs.

And stops at the open grave beside me.

The pallbearers all fall to their knees as if struck by a heavy blow to the back of their heads, the casket tips, the lid falls open and the dead fucking workman rolls out at my feet. He's wearing his blue cotton coveralls with "Property of the City of New Orleans, Public Works Dept" stamped in white paint across his chest.

A young woman in a white shroud breaks through the gaggle of mourners and throws herself, screaming, on top of the body. Two of the pallbearers drag the wailing angel away, and she collapses into the arms of the trombone player. The body is picked up, put gently back into the coffin, and the lid nailed shut again. The pallbearers lower the coffin into the grave, and it floats like a boat. The pastor begins to pray.

"O, remember that my life is wind . . . "

A heavy-set woman jumps into the grave, glances off the side of the coffin and falls down into the water. The gravedigger, naked except for a pair of ragged shorts, thrusts his shovel beneath her to keep her head out of the water and reaches down with both arms to pull her out with his hands around her neck. The woman is led away, and the procession departs, but not before each mourning woman picks a tuft of grass from the gravesite . . . *"When the saints go marching in"* . . . and the gravedigger gets to work with his shovel.

Ms Sugarlicq still sleeps on her slab.

"Everybody out."

It's the cemetery guard in green industrial slacks and long sleeve green shirt, and he's running here and there, up and down the rows of graves, down one walkway and up another, calling out for anyone in the cemetery to come to the main gate before locking it up for the night.

"Lock up."

The guard runs right past Ms Sugar, and she slowly stirs, yawning awake out of her deep sleep on top of the white marble slab. Stony with the discovery that marble is the alternative to consciousness, Ms S lingers as long as possible inside the high white walls of the cemetery. We ever so slowly make our way through the tombs to the exit.

A raucously brave graveyard bird, brown and white feathered, flatheaded and masked like a hangman, with two dark brown rings around the neck of its fat white body, scolds us from its perch on a heap of rubble at the gates.

"Everybody out."

Ms Sugarlicq and I turn off Basin onto St Louis Street, and are walking lakeside, looking for St Louis Cemetery No.2. It's the middle of the afternoon, deeper into The Projects, three kids, a girl and two boys bounce pass a basketball on the banquette half a block ahead. A police car jerks to a stop beside us, and the cop rolls down his window.

It's the lollipop cop.

"Where's your car parked?" he says.

"We don't have a car," I say.

"I advise you to avoid this neighbourhood," he says.

I can barely stand up.

Ms Sugar helps to hold me up.

"I can't guarantee your safety," he says.

I look down the street.

The girl makes a bounce pass to a boy.

She squeals.

It sounds like they're all singing, in perfect harmony, a rope-skipping song about blackbirds baked in a pie.

"What's the problem?" I say.

"Don't say I didn't warn you," he says.

"Wait," says Ms Sugarlicq.

She steps into the street.

"I'm going with you."

"You're going to leave me here?" I say.

"What?"

"I can barely fucking move."

"We're trying to build trust here," she says.

"Yeah right."

She gets into the police car, in the front seat beside the lollipop cop, and closes the door. The police car speeds away, lights flashing and siren wailing.

I was lying. I can still crawl.

New Year's Day, 1912, an eleven-year-old is arrested for firing a loaded gun in the middle of the street and sentenced to an orphanage. A year later, the shooting boy returns in triumph, blowing a blazing cornet, leading the Jones Colored Waifs' Home Band in a parade before ten thousand cheering people down Basin Street, the longest parade ever, going on to Chicago, New York, Paris, "Little Louis," the bringer of pure joy to the whole crazy world.

In the urban green, park bench peace of Louis Armstrong Park, the original Congo Square of voodoo dance and catgut song—and all that's left of legendary, honkytonk Storyville—I nap for a few minutes, fitful and nauseous, in the flowerbed beneath Louis's statue, a bare-headed, smiling, green brass, giant "Satchmo" with trumpet and handkerchief atop a cube of white stone.

But Louis could use a new suit. His right arm's beginning to corrode at the elbow, and you can see into the ragged, dark hollow of the brass casting. A family of ducks swims past in the park's dirty little pond, and I paddle along behind. A cop on horseback wakes me with a stick.

Lafitte's Blacksmith Shop, built in the 1730s, is one of the oldest buildings in New Orleans. The pirate Jean Lafitte is said to have laundered his ill-gotten goods through the back door. Except for the restrooms, it's lit only by candlelight and someone tinkling on a piano. The third Abita Red helps me. I can raise my head from the table without fear of falling off my chair.

Across the street from the bar on Bourbon Street, a guy on a red bicycle falls down in front of a mule pulling a wagon. The wagon's front left wheel crushes the man's bicycle helmet like a melon, but the guy jumps to his feet, shakes hands with the muledriver, walks across the street and sits down directly across at my open table just inside the cool darkness of the bar.

It's Paul.

His jaw is broken, and words tumble out of his mouth like pieces of bone.

"What are you trying to prove?" I say.

"Sold all the T-shirts," he says.

"Yeah right."

"None of us know what's in store for us and maybe it's a good thing that we don't," he says.

"I regret that I was ever born," I say.

"The best we can do is take it one day at a time," he says.

Out on the street, the brass band from the cemetery marches down Bourbon Street.

> *" . . . I'll be glad when you're dead,*
> *You rascal, you . . . "*

"That's my cue," says Paul.

"Yeah right."

And he's gone to dance down the street behind the band.

The Ferry to Algiers

Like a broken-necked, puppet Arlequin, I sit on the curb of
the banquette in front of the Voodoo Museum on Dumaine
Street. Head between knees, vomit on my shoes. The nails
of my rattling nerves hammer, and I fall backwards, swallowing my tongue and the chewy, grislier bits of indignity. I
swim through dense, hardening shit, in the darkest reaches
of the sour belly, and eat it, greasy with raw, rapacious greed.

I'm picked up by the armpits and wobble dangerously,
uncontrollably lurch about the banquette, swinging back
and forth, barely touching the pavement on my tiptoes. I do
a quick, short choreographed dance. I bow. My arms flail like
semaphores, my double-jointed knees jerk repeatedly up
and down. I do the splits twice, am turned completely
around in a circle three times and then pushed hard from
behind through the doorway into the tiny vestibule of the
Voodoo Museum.

The front room of the museum is a souvenir shop selling
voodoo dolls fashioned from scraps of cotton and yellow
straw; black, yellow, red, and green crucifixes, plastercast
Virgin Marys, painted snakes carved from wood into walking
sticks, vodu idols, pipes, bowls, postcards, black and white
lithographs of Congo Square, Saint John's Eve, Marie Laveau,

the "Widow of Paris"..."*the Vaudoux Queen madly dances betwixt joy and woe with her hair on fire*"... aluminum Mardi Gras doubloons, baubles, strings of glass beads, candles to ward off evil spirits and demons, hand-stitched, pocketless funeral shrouds, witchcraft aids; Zapp's Potato Chips, Barq's Root Beer, voodoo chewing gum, Cuban cigars, one hundred and one varieties of Louisiana hot sauce, chicory coffee, pecan pralines, pirated cassette tape dubs of Dr John, hand-bound box-set voodoo biographies in red and black leather: *Jesus and Legba*; voodoo cookbooks ... "*if a woman adds her menstrual blood to a gumbo, her man will never stray; if she cuts his hair or clips his fingernails to thicken an etouffée, she will control his every move*" ... voodoo incense, voodoo medicinal herbs, voodoo powders, voodoo elixirs, voodoo potents, voodoo charms, amulets, talismans which are tiny pieces of paper marked with stick drawings of complex spiritualist symbolism rolled into scrolls the size of a cigarette and tied with a simple bow of red or black cotton string. Tucked into a small chamois bag, suspended by a cotton string, and worn around the neck so that it dangles loosely between the breasts, the talisman protects you from ever falling in love.

I discover Ms Sugarlicq purchasing a talisman from Madame L, *tall and elegant, well proportioned, slim waist line, the most beautiful woman in New Orleans*, and who happens to be talking about hair.

"Her hair is brown," she says to Ms Sugar. "Brown, but she thinks she's a blonde. But she isn't blonde, she's brown. I say, get over it, you're brown, but she gets her hair dyed anyway. She says, what do you think? I say that's not blonde, it's yellow."

I tap Ms Sugar on the shoulder.

She turns around, the talisman dangling between her breasts. Without making eye contact, she walks towards the door.

"Baby," I say.

Tinkle . . . she goes out the door and disappears in the sudden heat from the street.

"She don't see you no more," says Madame L.

"Yeah right."

There's an effigy doll, fashioned from straw and crudely sewn cheap cotton, on the mahogany counter between us. The doll has a miniature trumpet case clutched in its straw arms. Madame L raises the left leg of the doll and turns it toward the door.

I turn and goose step to the door.

"Yeah right," says Madame L.

I find Ms Sugarlicq eating an ice cream cone by the fountain in the garden courtyard of Le Petit Theatre du Vieux Carré. A rehearsal of Carlo Gozzi's *Turandot* is in progress in the theatre.

"Talk to me."

Ms S finishes her cone, wipes her mouth with a paper napkin, puts on lipstick, but she won't talk, won't even look at me. I, wretched dog, curl up in a ball at her feet, and she stands up and steps over me, walking away. Her high heels click, and in the theatre the guillotine drops.

A busker brass band of beat-up tuba, washboard, two trombones and a clarinet set fire to Jackson Square in the swelling afternoon. I slump on the blazing steps in front of St Louis Cathedral and shiver in the heat. Ms S walks by, keeps walking, and I follow, limping behind, calling out her name, my voice high-pitched and cracking, afraid of losing her in the crowd.

On the ferry to Algiers, I follow her onboard. She meets a dealer from the casino in a thousand dollar suit, gold cufflinks, watch and ring, who asks me, like a total stranger, to take their picture, and Ms S cuddles up close beside him. In the viewfinder, they look like a couple on their honeymoon.

The dealer thanks me, and returning the camera, Ms S turns away as if I didn't exist. I follow behind as the two of them stroll arm in arm around the deck. Time zones away across the water in the wake of the ferry, the whole French Quarter in sun jewel miniature floats, rosette, above the wide, muddy river, *waters rolling down from mid-America like the torrent of broken souls.* Sometimes the river sounds like a lover taking off her clothes for another man.

I go up to them sharing a bench and ask the dealer if he knows the house where William Burroughs lived in Algiers, and he gives me directions.

The three of us walk off the ferry landing together and down the hill to the swinging door of the Dry Dock Café and Bar where Ms S freezes on the banquette as the dealer slips through the door into cool darkness.

"Are we going in here?" I say.

She turns around and starts walking back up the levee.

"I thought we were going to look for Burroughs's house."

She keeps walking up the levee.

I let her go.

She sits down on a bench at the top.

I walk up from behind.

"You just want to sit here?"

She turns her head away.

I set my battered trumpet case down on the bench beside her and walk the levee banquette a quarter mile or so to a large complex of warehouses with a sign that says *Mardi Gras World.* Tethered to the fence in the yard, leering at me, a gargoyle's head as big as a house. I turn away, walk and then run down the steep levee to the river, stepping into soft mud to pick a nosegay of black-eyed Susans growing wild. I take off my shoes and socks and wade into the hyacinths.

"Freeze."

The lollipop cop stands over me with police issue revolver drawn. He takes one step into the shallows. I pull up a hyacinth by the roots, and the lollipop cop slips, losing his balance backwards into two inches of water. I grab the heels of his boots and drag him thrashing into the deeper muddy. Like an evil twin, I pounce upon his torso, and wrestling the revolver away, pistol-whip him until his head drops into the water like a heavy stone. A small patch of the brown river shallows in the blue hyacinths bubbles red, and the lollipop cop's waterlogged body floats away, bobbing through the hyacinths into the larger stream, swirling.

What would Burroughs do?

I walk back along the levee banquette, the sun a bleeding heart above the Vieux Carré, and a crooked, reflected rail of sunlight like shining blood divides the river. I walk all the way back to Ms Sugarlicq sitting on the bench, looking at the sunset, not looking at me, and I shoot her pointblank between the eyes.

I drop the bouquet of black-eyed Susans on the body. The flower stem tie breaks, and the flowers blow, strewing here and there across her face and along the banquette.

I scramble down the levee over big white rocks and throw the revolver, bouncing once, a flash of steel like a skipping stone, into the brown, swirling water.

I pick up the trumpet and take the next return ferry to New Orleans.

I get a table with a white linen tablecloth in a bay window looking out on St Louis Street at the Gumbo Shop and eat a full-course Creole supper of salad, greens, soup, mache corn, chicken Creole, crawfish gumbo, white rice and red beans, bread pudding, brownie pie, and Abita beer.

I walk down Pirate's Alley to the Faulkner Bookstore and buy a first edition hardback copy of Nelson Algren's *A Walk on the Wild Side* for sixty dollars American.

I have a chicory café au lait and a plate of hot beignets at Café du Monde and watch the passing scene, the whole human comedy dancing in camellia neon New Orleans after dark.

I check the time, and my wristwatch is disintegrating, the leather band falling away in rot, and insects run across the dial. I look back up across the street, and wandering through the mixing crowd in a sleepwalking daze is Ms Sugarlicq.

I jump to my feet, knocking a chair over, and run into the street, trying to untangle from another second chair as I fall down headfirst, my chin skidding across the pavement.

Honk . . .

I turn my head up from the pavement of Decatur Street in time to see Doc and the horror on his face, through the windshield behind the wheel of his Datsun, as he runs over me.

I lie on my back in the middle of the street with my body ripped open like a plastic bag, the sour sewage of my insides spreading. Dark blood burbles in pumping clots from my mouth. Hovering above me are two angels: Paul, his head crushed and jaw broken, and Ms Sugarlicq, the bullet hole neat and tidy and deeper than I ever imagined between her eyes. She has woven a tiara of black-eyed Susans through her golden hair.

"Why aren't I dead?" I say.

"You are dead," says Paul.

"Yeah right."

"You've been dead for some time," he says.

My trumpet lies beside me crushed as if run over by a car.

Ms S leans down to kiss me on the lips.

"I love you," she says.

"I love you, too."

Taking my last breath, I feel a boner coming on.

There's a big parade down Frenchmen Street, and a big crowd lines both sides of the street to cheer the marching jass band passing by. Leading the band in a diamond formation are four brass horns: Buddy Bolden struts out front with his blazing cornet, Kid Ory on valve trombone and Louis Armstrong on cornet march side by side, swinging, and I follow behind, Lewis "Sweet Horn" King, trying my best to keep up, playing the trumpet. Our horns are sweet, we always have sweet horns, and the crowd goes crazy, buying us three-for-one drinks, and we play:

> *"Going to New Orleans*
> *To blow my bell,*
> *Going to New Orleans*
> *Going to hell."*

THE END.

Piracy

Page 55: "a look of belonging there as has the flush upon sunset clouds" —Mark Twain, *Life on the Mississippi*.

Page 63: "my head buzzing with a sound like a downed wire in a rain puddle." —James Lee Burke, *Purple Cane Road*.

Page 74: "like a tearing of endless silk" —William Faulkner, *Mosquitoes*.

Page 80: "And down the long unshaded street a vendor of colored ices beat a rainbow of tin bells." —Nelson Algren, *A Walk on the Wild Side*.

Page 85: "I strode resolutely across town, thankful that I was still alive." —John Kennedy Toole, *A Confederacy of Dunces*.

Page 90: "deepening to purple over the river." —Anne Rice, *Feast of All Saints*.

Page 90: "laughing all around us in the dusk." —Sherwood Anderson, "A Meeting South."

Page 91: "Topless dancers, strippers, drag queens, B-girls, waiters, bartenders, and the hoarse-voiced doormen barkers." —Truman Capote, *Music for Chameleons*.

Page 103: "bury my nose in that snowy expanse of soft finespun cotton." —Walker Percy, *The Moviegoer*.

Page 122: "a little piece of eternity dropped into your hands—and who knows what to do with it?" —Tennessee Williams, *A Streetcar Named Desire*.

Page 134: "All in New Orleans are buried in water." —Benjamin H.B. Latrobe, *Impressions Respecting New Orleans*.

Page 140: "tall and elegant, well proportioned, slim waist line, the most beautiful woman in New Orleans" —Helen d'Aquin Allain, *Memoirs*.

Page 142: "waters rolling down from mid-America like the torrent of broken souls" —Jack Kerouac, *On the Road*.

About the Author

Charles Tidler's stage plays have been produced throughout Canada, in Los Angeles, New York, and London's West End. They have won many awards and honors. Charles is also a poet and a spoken jazz artist. *Going to New Orleans* is his first novel.